Cover Illustration by Piet

The Witch's Bargain

Penny and John
And One-Eyed Zach
And the Witch in the House
On Postman's Hack

A. T. Salem

For Liesbeth, Pieter, and Erick
and Seth, the boy next door,
Who all may remember

Find three in the sea where you lose your
direction

*

Three there in the air where you swirl all
direction

*

Fields of rubies hide buried treasure
Where the lighthouse disappears

*

*

Do not hold onto what you find first

*

Time gives golden treasures
When it is time

One Wet Afternoon

It was raining when Penny and John climbed into the car.

"Don't touch anything," Mrs. Collins told Penny, as if she ever would.

"Don't kick my seat," Mrs. Collins told John before he even thought of it. "You don't know how much I hate children."

Penny and John hated Mrs. Collins. They hated her car, which smelled as if she dusted it with cigarette ashes. They hated her clothes, which looked as if she wore them to bed. But most of all, they hated her. She was lazy and grumpy, and she always sounded as if she had peas in her nose. She looked like it, too, with nostrils that flared open when she breathed. John called Mrs. Collins a Hairy Boar and Penny drew pictures of her scorched with purple dragon fire. Mrs. Collins never knew about the pictures. She never guessed about the nickname. It didn't matter. She wouldn't have cared.

"I don't want to hear a peep out of you, Missy." Mrs. Collins adjusted her mirror before she started the engine. "It's bad enough having to drive in this weather."

Rain fell in hard, bitter pellets as they crossed the bridge out of town. When they drove past strawberry fields, it came down like steel-cold nails. By the time they could see gray ocean again, rain swept over the windows like curtains. Penny and John wondered if it was the most miserable day ever and Mrs. Collins was sure it was. She growled all the way up the last hill and growled when she turned off the car and growled when she couldn't find her umbrella.

"What an awful day," Mrs. Collins said and sneezed without covering her mouth.

Penny and John didn't say anything. They looked up at a house sagging into the ground like a plastic bag in a puddle. In the mud, John noticed a rock carved like a gravestone:

47
Postman's Hack Road

Safe Haven, Maine

"Welcome to your new home," Mrs. Collins said. Thunder rumbled.

One First Step

The house was the color of old wood, grayer than the sky. The windows hid underneath eaves like sparrows trying to stay dry. High on the roof, a chimney wobbled as the wind blew. The wind made a low, sighing sound.

Mrs. Collins turned around in her seat. "What are you waiting for, Missy, a red carpet? Get out of the car."

Penny and John opened their doors. A car splashed past and soaked Penny's jeans. John stepped into a stream sweeping over the gutter. Lightning flashed.

2

"Stop right there, Buster." Mrs. Collins slammed her car door. "I told you to wait. No running away this time."

John looked at Penny and Penny looked at the road. She hesitated too long and Mrs. Collins had time to grab John's wrist. She tried to reach Penny's, but Penny pulled it away too quickly. "Fine." Mrs. Collins shook her umbrella so that it dribbled rain down John's neck. "If that's the impression you want to give her, that's fine with me."

Thunder boomed.

Mrs. Collins dragged John to the porch and pressed the doorbell. "Don't start anything," Mrs. Collins told Penny as she climbed up the steps. "You don't want her to change her mind."

John slipped away and stood with Penny on the edge of the porch. She glanced down at his feet, where a wet sock poked through a hole in his sneakers. Penny knew he was too small and too skinny, but his eyes were big and brown and sad. John wanted a family more than anything else, but his sister was all he had.

As he put on the sweatshirt, John saw Penny clench her fists to keep from shivering. He and Penny had the same round cheeks and the same dark hair, but Penny had muscles and bruises and wary, watchful eyes. She knew she had to be careful. She knew she had to be smart. She'd made a promise to look after her brother and Penny kept her promises. Her brother was all she had.

Lightning struck.

"She must be here," Mrs. Collins muttered, pressing the doorbell again. Her umbrella tapped impatiently on a muddy welcome mat. Nothing happened. She banged on the front door and nothing happened. The boards under their feet sank with little cracking sounds. Still, nothing happened.

"This is ridiculous." Mrs. Collins swung around to jab her umbrella at Penny. "If you can't stay here, Missy, I'm going to have to take you to that girl's home. And what I'm going to do with you, Buster, I don't know. It'll have to be another night at the shelter." Mrs. Collins peered through a window by the door. "There's no other place that can take the two of you together. You're trouble like we've never seen before —"

The door creaked open.

Penny and John cocked their heads. Mrs. Collins turned around. She opened her mouth to say something rude, but not a word came out.

There was nobody there.

Thunder rumbled again.

"Hm," Mrs. Collins said.

But there wasn't a sound from inside.

"Hello?"

No answer.

"I can't believe this." Mrs. Collins took a strong hold of her umbrella and knocked it against the doorway. "Miss McKinney, I am wet and tired, and here with the children you wanted. Take them now or they'll leave with me."

Suddenly, the wind rose, sweeping over their backs, through the door and inside the house. Just as quickly, the wind returned. With it came a voice.

One Dusty Room

"Hello!" the voice called. "You are early. Come in!"

Mrs. Collins peered forward. "Miss McKinney?"

But the voice didn't answer.

4

"Humph," Mrs. Collins said. She marched forward a step, reached back and yanked both Penny and John's hands. "You heard her."

The door slammed shut behind them.

Penny and John looked around. They stood in a hallway so dark they could barely see the staircase drooping against a wall. The ceiling shivered puffs of dust down to the floor. Penny took a step behind Mrs. Collins. John followed, ready to dash to the door if Penny gave the sign. Before Penny could, lightening flashed, illuminating the living room through an archway. Ghostly shadows looked down from paintings on the walls.

"Don't dawdle," Mrs. Collins said. She shoved the children to a lumpy sofa by a rocking chair and a crumbling fireplace. When they sat down, the cushions billowed more dust into their noses. John had to hold his breath to keep from sneezing.

"Stop fidgeting," Mrs. Collins said.

Behind them, with deep, hollow ticks, a clock counted the time around dusty numbers: 1 through 28. When his legs started to fall asleep, John swung his feet, but Mrs. Collins jabbed a finger in his side to make him stop. Penny looked at the empty fireplace and shivered. She wished it weren't so cold.

Thunder shook the walls. John yawned.

All of a sudden, the clocked whirred into motion. Four bells pinged the hour and the clock creaked to life. Two little men danced through the doors in the clock. They whirled and twirled and hit one another over the head with little silver crescents in their hands. Then they whirled and twirled back inside their doors.

Mrs. Collins grunted and picked up her bag from the floor. She didn't see the black cat lying on the roof

5

of the clock. The cat stared at them with one eye closed and one green eye glittering. Then he winked – John was sure he winked – and leaped to the floor.

A woman stood beside the fireplace.

"Finally," Mrs. Collins said. "Miss McKinney, these are the Martinez children." She poked John to make him sit up straight. "Children, this is Miss McKinney."

"Abigail," the woman said, holding out her hand. "Please call me Abigail. And pardon me for keeping you waiting. I was trying to bake scones and the oven was very difficult."

Mrs. Collins ignored her hand. "We haven't got all day, you know."

"Of course." Abigail put her hand in her pocket as if she didn't know what else to do.

"Mrrow," said the cat from beneath the sofa.

Abigail blinked. "Yes," she said, "Tea." She pulled a cart from behind her. A teapot sat beside cupcakes, mugs and a steaming pitcher of hot chocolate. Abigail glanced at Mrs. Collins. "I hope the cupcakes are all right. I had to rush and I am afraid they got wet on the way. But they came from a good bakery in town."

Mrs. Collins opened her bag and pulled out a stack of forms. "I really don't have the time."

"Oh," Abigail said. "Naturally. I understand."

Thunder boomed.

Abigail looked at Penny and John. "You will take something, I hope. There are chocolate and vanilla cupcakes, and some even have frosting. I was not sure which you would like." She blinked and looked surprised. "You are cold – cold and wet straight through. We should have a fire."

She reached into the fireplace and rearranged ashy pieces of wood. Blue and orange flames darted into the

6

chimney and out again. In the light, Abigail's face turned a sick, greenish color.

"That will warm you up." Abigail sat in the rocking chair. "Penelope Rose, would you pour your brother some hot chocolate? And Mrs. Collins, shall you pass the cupcakes?"

Mrs. Collins snorted. "This is a waste of time." She waved the handfuls of papers at Abigail. "I need you to sign these. Then I'll be on my way."

Lightning flashed.

"John Tomas, will you be so kind as to pass the cakes?" Abigail tried smiling at Penny. "And would you pour me some tea? Milk only, please."

Penny slowly filled a teacup with tea that shimmered golden. John took a cupcake. Mrs. Collins tapped her toes.

"Thank you, Penelope Rose." Abigail sipped her tea. "This is perfect."

"Really, Miss McKinney," Mrs. Collins said, sounding even more like she had peas in her nose. "These children hardly need –"

"Mrs. Collins, you must take something." Abigail set her teacup in its saucer with a clink. "John Tomas, do you see a chocolate cupcake?"

Mrs. Collins took the one with the most frosting. "I don't think you understand, Miss McKinney," she said with her mouth full of cupcake. "These children don't need treats. They need structure and discipline. Nobody knows a thing about their father. Their mother kept them in motel rooms before she got sick. They've been to eight schools in the past three years and they've had trouble in every one. We're lucky they can even read."

Thunder grumbled outside.

Abigail tried to cut in. "I do not think – "

"Missy here has gotten into twenty fistfights since we've had her. The counselor can't get a word out of the boy. These children won't understand kindness. They'd abuse it."

"Yet with a fresh start —"

"They're bound for prison, Miss McKinney — prison or drug addiction or alcohol abuse." Mrs. Collins took a last bite of cupcake. "Then they'll probably die like their mother."

Beneath the sofa, the cat hissed. Lightning flashed through the windows. A draft swept over their shoulders. And Mrs. Collins began coughing. She began gasping. She gagged and wheezed and waved her hands in the air. "I'm – choking!" she croaked.

Abigail took another sip of tea. "Yes, that can happen," she said. "You should not speak with your mouth full."

Mrs. Collins' nose turned red. Her face turned blue. John thought she might really be in trouble, but with a clap of lightning, the fire leaped high again. A gooey blob of cupcake shot out of Mrs. Collins' mouth and landed beside the sugar bowl.

The cat curled a tail around John's ankle.

"Much better." Abigail held out her cup. "Penelope Rose, I will take a second cup of tea, if you please."

John noticed that Mrs. Collins' hands were shaking as she wiped her nose on her sleeve. "I just meant that you don't know what the children need," she said.

"But I have read all sorts of books." Abigail accepted her cup back from Penny. "And the children will help, I am sure. Come any time and you will see how we are getting along."

Thunder rumbled out to sea.

"Fine." Mrs. Collins brushed crumbs onto Penny's lap. "Sign the papers and the children are yours. In the meantime, Missy, you go get your things from the car."

"You do not think the children should go out in this weather, do you?" Abigail found an emerald green pen in her hair. "Their clothes will be dry in a moment."

"Humph," said Mrs. Collins. She picked up her umbrella, and then looked over her nose at Penny and John. "I expect you two to behave properly. You've got school tomorrow and then the weekend to get yourselves organized. But hear this, Missy: one bad report and you'll go to that girls' home faster than you can wave bye-bye to your baby brother."

"I am certain you will hear only good things." Abigail moved Mrs. Collins towards the hall. She nodded to the cat on the floor. "Help them feel at home, Squint."

Squint yawned and flicked his tail at her.

Penny and John waited until they heard the front door slam. Then Penny made a face. "She calls us by our whole names," she said. "It's stupid."

"She has a cat," John whispered. "I like cats."

Penny looked at Squint. He had a fat belly and a squashed face covered in old scars. Only one eye could open and it stared at her.

"Dogs are better," Penny said.

Squint stalked away with his tail in the air.

Lightning lit the floor behind him.

One Introduction

In the hallway, they could hear Mrs. Collins complaining as she dropped their bags. They heard her stomp down the porch stairs and slam her car door. Outside, the foghorn cooed. The walls of the house settled back as the wind swirled away. John edged closer to Penny on the sofa.

"It certainly is wet out there," Abigail said on her way into the room. "Have you dried out? Perhaps you should have more hot chocolate. John Tomas, please fill your cup." She sat down in her rocking chair. "And Penelope Rose, you too, if you like."

Penny was full, but she poured more cocoa for John. Neither of them spoke.

"Well," Abigail said.

The children didn't say a word.

"Hm," Abigail said.

Abigail looked funny, John thought. She had a nose that turned up, eyes that turned down and a mouth that couldn't seem to decide which way to turn and just stayed crooked. Her fingers were longer than they ought to have been and her legs were too long for the chair. Penny wondered if Abigail had enough to eat. Maybe that was why she was skinny and sallow.

"Eat another cupcake," Penny whispered to John. They might need to store up their energy.

"There are some other things to eat, too, if you like," Abigail said. "Peanut butter and milk and breakfast cereal and…" She bit her lip. "You do eat cereal, I hope. I have six different kinds. But I also have oatmeal. And cream of wheat. I was not sure which you might want."

Penny shrugged. John looked at the fire. Thunder grumbled, but this time from further away. John shivered.

"Well," Abigail said.

John started kicking his legs. Penny nudged his thigh to make him stop.

"Perhaps you would like to hear some things about me," Abigail said. "That might help. You must be curious."

Penny and John didn't say anything.

"My name is Abigail, but then you already know that. And I know that you, Penelope Rose, are eleven and in fifth grade. And John Tomas, you are eight and in second grade." She hesitated. "I know that your mother could not take care of you easily, but you both cooked and cleaned and looked after her as if you were grown up. I heard you were very brave when she died."

Penny and John looked at the floor. They didn't want to talk about their mother.

"I am sorry," Abigail said. "What you have suffered is unforgettable. But I hope I can make it easier to remember. You will have to teach me a great deal, since I have never had children before. Still, I hope I can help."

Squint sauntered past the couch and squatted where he could get a good look at the children. "Mrrow," he declared.

"You have a cat," Penny said. She didn't care that her voice sounded sullen.

"Do not mind him if he is a bother. Once he sees how lovely you are, I am sure you will get along well enough." Abigail attempted a smile, but John noticed that she pushed the cat away with her foot.

"It's an ugly cat," Penny told her.

With a saucy look at Penny, Squint lifted a hind leg.

"None of that." Abigail picked the cat up and dropped him on the rocking chair. "Shall we go upstairs? You must want to get settled."

11

Penny shrugged. John stood up. Squint settled himself into the chair and watched them go with one cold, green eye.

One Trip Upstairs

The floorboards sank with every step they climbed upstairs. The walls groaned whenever the wind blew. At the landing, Abigail flicked on a light switch. Single bulbs flickered from a chandelier and one bulb gave up with a pop, showering glass onto the staircase. John reached for Penny's hand.

"You can pick any room you like." Abigail walked down the hallway opening doors to show their options. "My things are in the attic. I will keep that door locked most of the time, since everything is lying about and I do not want you to hurt yourselves. In the evening, of course, you may knock if you need me. The stairs at the end of the hall lead down to the kitchen and that door there is for the bathroom. I know it is not pretty now, but I thought you could decide how to arrange things. Separate rooms or together, whichever you like. Once you choose, we could begin to fix them up. All my books say children like to control their environment."

Penny pushed open the first door. She found a large room with a big window overlooking the street. But the room contained nothing else except a metal cot and one long, coffee-colored stain from the ceiling.

Beside it, John found a small room with a metal cot and a dresser standing on three legs. He snapped on the light switch and sparks shot out from the socket hanging from the ceiling. He didn't say anything. He didn't move. He stood frozen, staring at the room.

The toilet in the small bathroom gurgled when Penny came down the hallway. A third bedroom had a broken pair of cots and a set of moldy books on an old shelf. Beetles scuttled into closets. Cobwebs hung over windows. Penny thought of the shelter, which at least had furniture in bright colors. She thought of the times they'd slept in sour-smelling hospital rooms or on musty motel beds. They had never stayed in a place so filthy. She turned around.

"This is it?" she asked and felt her cheeks getting hot.

"Ye-es." Abigail hesitated. "We will rearrange things, of course. The people who used to live here did not care for the house and I never could figure out what to do first. I thought I would wait until you said what you needed. What do you think?"

Penny could have cried, but she didn't. Instead, she got mad. She clenched her teeth to keep from saying something that would get them into trouble. She tried to take deep breaths to stay calm. Nothing worked. "I can't believe it." Penny turned around, seeing muddy splatters across the windows and dark stains on the mattresses.

Penny swung around again and this time, she knocked the books to the floor. She was getting so angry, she couldn't see clearly. "I can't believe it," she repeated, louder and louder until her throat hurt. "I can't believe it. I can't believe they left us here with you. I can't believe it!"

Abigail's eyes grew wide and worried. "I did not think… That is, I did plan on making changes. Perhaps not immediately, but I will try." She took a deep breath. "What do you need most of all?"

"Look at this!" Penny stomped into the next bedroom. "This is worse than a prison cell. There's nothing here. Where are we supposed to put our clothes? How are we going to sleep without sheets? It was better at the homeless shelter." She stomped over to the bathroom. "We don't even have a shower. Look at it! Does the water run at all? I can't believe this!"

Penny flung herself into the room where John still hadn't moved. "John," she said, not even bothering to whisper. "I promised Mom that I would take care of you and I promise you I will. We're going to get out of here as soon as we can – even if I have to call the Hairy Boar."

"Penelope Rose," Abigail stood in the doorway. She looked as if she were about to cry. "Really, I did not expect you to be upset. They never said – my books never said I – I am sorry. I promise things will be better tomorrow." She knelt by John and took his hand. "John Tomas, just tell me what you want."

"I want my mom!" John whipped his hand away and ran to the front room.

"I hate you!" Penny ran after him and slammed the door.

Later, neither of the children came out when Abigail called them for dinner. They didn't come out to get their bags and pajamas. They fell asleep on the cot with the dark stain and damp smell. The hush of the rain hid the click of the door as Abigail came to put blankets over their shoulders.

One New Morning

Penny felt sunshine on her face, but she didn't want to open her eyes. Even in her sleep, she'd dreamed of all the things she had to worry about: the cot, the water stain, the dirty, empty room and the old, dusty house. They had a new skinny guardian, a scabby black cat, Mrs. Collins' threats, and only the start of a plan to run away. But at the end of the bed, Penny heard John snoring. Penny had promised to take care of her brother. It was time to wake up and start.

Penny sighed and opened her eyes.

She blinked.

She opened her eyes wider and sat up.

"John," she said. "You've got to see."

John rolled over into a soft, plush pillow. He mumbled something and pulled a fuzzy blanket over his shoulders. Then he realized he had a soft stuffed animal in the crook of his arm. John opened his eyes.

"Isn't it – wow?" Penny asked.

The dirty, empty room had vanished. In its place was a bedroom full and green like a jungle. Penny and John sat on one fat bed. Its twin lay alongside piled high with blue pillows. Along the walls, little dog statues supported stacks of books. Below the windows, plush dogs sat on toy trucks and trains.

15

John rubbed his eyes.

A pair of desks had leaping puppies on drawers and shelves all the way to the ceiling. A thick rug had multi-colored puppies rolling around on the floor.

Gingerly, Penny touched the pink fur on a tiny stuffed poodle. "How did she do it?"

"I hope you do not mind." Abigail stood in the shadows of the doorway. "I took a chance on the color. But I heard you say that you liked dogs, Penelope Rose. And your backpacks are green. It is not too much, is it?"

"Too much?" Penny stared at her.

Abigail took a step forward. "Perhaps I should have waited to ask what you wanted, but when you seemed so unhappy and ready to leave, I thought I should try." She hesitated. "The books said children liked surprises."

John was so confused that he couldn't even nod. Then he smelled the air. Something was burning.

Abigail clapped her hand to her mouth. "My pancakes!" She darted down the hallway.

Penny looked after her. Abigail's footprints stood out in the dust on the floor. Cobwebs wafted in the doorway. Except for their bedroom, nothing in the house had changed.

"How did Abigail do all this while we were sleeping?" Penny asked.

John looked at their clothes hanging in the closet. He saw their pictures with their mother hanging on the wall. As he climbed off the bed, the rug beneath his feet felt soft and silky. The sun shone bright and clean through the windows.

"I don't get it," John said. "There was nothing here yesterday."

"I don't trust it," Penny said. Normal rooms wouldn't transform overnight, not without waking them up. Penny climbed off the bed. "We'd better get dressed. And be ready to run if we need to leave fast. Something weird is going on and I don't like that one bit."

One Burned Breakfast

Outside their new room, the house was as dusty and dirty as they had remembered. Spiders dropped from the ceiling to watch them make their way down the hallway. A soft whoosh of dust fell to the floor as they walked down the stairs. As the clock pinged seven times, John noticed the little men held bigger crescents than the day before.

"Penny," John started to say.

"Back here," Abigail called. "In the kitchen."

A film of flour covered the floor. The oven coughed out enough smoke to fill the ceiling. On a wobbly table beneath a window, chipped dishes sat crowded by boxes of cereal, bowls of fruit, and pitchers of milk and juice.

"Good morning," Abigail said brightly. "I thought you might be hungry since you had no dinner last night. There are plenty of choices – except no pancakes. They burned so badly I had to throw them away. Perhaps Squint will pick them out of the garbage. But there are sausages on the table somewhere. Please help yourself."

John wrinkled his nose. Something still didn't smell right.

Abigail didn't look right either. "Your face is green," Penny said.

"I am not used to cooking. And the oven refuses to cooperate. But the stove seems to be cooking the grits properly. The eggs I have boiled for half an hour and I cannot determine if they have cooked enough. Would you like to try them?"

On the counter, John saw charred crumbles of toast. Penny noticed something orange oozing out the bottom of a can. "We'll have cereal," she said.

"Cereal it is." Abigail handed John big yellow mixing bowls and a pair of wooden spoons. "And what would you like me to pack for your lunch? I have peanut butter and turkey and tuna...."

"It doesn't matter. Whatever." Penny looked for normal cereal bowls, but there weren't any.

"Lunch is easy then. But difficult, too. Do you like bananas? What about peaches?"

John reached for the pitcher of juice and then changed his mind. The juice was brown and chunky.

"I could make a salad," Abigail said, reaching for a jar of peanut butter. "That is, I believe I could make a salad. Actually, I have never made a salad, but I am sure I could figure it out if you wanted one as a snack. Or perhaps you do not like vegetables. My books say that children can be picky."

"Abigail," Penny interrupted, "nobody puts mayonnaise on a peanut butter sandwich."

"Are you sure? What about mustard?"

Penny and John looked at one another. Did Abigail really not know how to make a sandwich?

"You're supposed to use jelly," Penny said. "That's why it's called a peanut butter and jelly sandwich."

"Of course. Jelly and peanut butter. I am sure I have jelly somewhere." As Abigail rummaged through a cupboard, the wind blew the back door open.

With a bang, the door slammed shut again. John jumped.

There in front of him were two jars of grape jelly.

Penny lifted the box of cereal that had fallen over. "The jelly is right here," she said.

But the grape jelly had not been there when they'd sat down. He would have noticed. Thinking hard, John stared out the window. There was something strange going on.

Penny thought so, too, as she watched Abigail shake pepper over the peanut butter. "Haven't you ever made a sandwich before?"

"No." Abigail sprinkled parsley over the pepper. "And I looked in my books and none of them gave any recipes."

"But you made hot chocolate yesterday and the cupcakes were decent." Penny stopped. "Or did you buy everything from a store?"

"In a way." Abigail looked guilty.

"I would have thought Mrs. Collins would have checked you out more. At least to see if you could cook."

John stopped listening to Penny. Beneath a pine tree out the kitchen window, a robin searched for worms. It didn't notice Squint crouched low in a tuft of grass. Without moving a blade, Squint inched closer and closer.

Abigail flew to the table and banged at the window. "Squint, you leave him alone!"

Squint pounced, but too late. The robin had already escaped to the pine tree. As the robin twittered down at him, Squint spat back at Abigail.

"You have good senses, John Tomas." Abigail pressed her lips together as the cat lifted his tail. "Horrid cat."

Squint made a rude noise and walked away.

"Squint doesn't care what you think," Penny said.

"Squint never cares what anyone thinks." Abigail stopped and sniffed the air.

John looked around at the stove.

"Grits? Oops – I forgot!" She leapt back to the stove to snatch a smoking pan off a burner. "What awful luck I am having this morning. And you, John Tomas, have saved the day again." She poked a finger inside the pot. "Are the grits supposed to be black?"

She looked over at the table, only to catch Penny rolling her eyes. "Oh." Abigail's shoulders drooped. "You do not want to try them? There is bacon."

"We can't eat bacon raw."

Abigail sighed again. "I suppose Squint might eat grits, too."

John didn't think so. Squint had disappeared over the old stones of an old garden wall.

Penny went back to her cereal. "I think Squint's a stupid name," she said.

"Do you?" Abigail began slicing peaches. "He complains about it, too."

John looked up. "He does?"

Penny rolled her eyes. "Like cats can talk."

"Squint does not need to talk in order to share his opinion, John Tomas. Just listen to him out there." Abigail winced as a yowl rose up through the pine trees. "The neighbors complain, but he pays no attention. He wakes them up with yodeling, and when they go to bed at night, he practices battle cries. He is dreadful."

20

"Why don't you get rid of him?" Penny asked. "Get a dog or something if you want a real pet."

"I have considered it." Abigail used a hairbrush to wipe her knife clean. "But unfortunately, Squint is relying on me. I took him on as my responsibility, so now I have to look after him, however little I want to."

Squint's yowling grew louder, but Abigail shook herself. "If you are through eating, you had better hurry and brush your teeth and things. They told me to have you at school early to meet your teachers. You do brush your teeth after breakfast, I hope. All my books said brushing after meals is important."

"I don't know what the Hairy Board was thinking by leaving us here," Penny told John upstairs in the bathroom. Pipes clanked like wind chimes as they brushed their teeth. The toilet burbled at them as they wiped their faces. "Everything is messed up. Nothing works right. Abigail can't expect to get everything fixed all of a sudden, no matter how quickly she cleaned up our room. I don't get it."

"And did you see? The jelly wasn't on the table when we sat down."

"No time for talking, John Tomas," Abigail called up the stairs. "I have your lunches in your bags already. We will need to walk quickly to get to school."

Back downstairs, Abigail handed them their backpacks and hurried them through the back door.

"But how did you clean the kitchen so fast?" John asked, turning from the door to stare. The flour had vanished, along with the smoke and the dirty dishes. For a second, it seemed as if a towel were wiping out the sink by itself. John blinked and the towel was draped over the faucet.

"Just out the back here, John Tomas." Abigail hurried him outside. She closed the door to the kitchen firmly behind him.

One Maine Morning

Penny and John followed Abigail through the weedy remains of a garden.

"Don't you have a car?" Penny asked.

"No." Abigail stopped to wrap a purple scarf around her neck. "And I have no idea how to drive, even if I had one. Luckily, we are not too far away from everything. We could meet the bus to go in town just out the front door. And you can walk to school on the path back here. Just climb over the stone wall, John Tomas, and look at your state of Maine. You could not be in a prettier spot."

They stepped out of the shadows of the pine trees and into clear sunshine. Before them, a gravel path skirted black rocks and blue ocean. The water glittered with sparkles of yellow gold around islands spiked with pine trees. John stopped watching his feet and wrinkled his nose. The wind blew salty and crisp.

"What a perfect morning." Abigail stopped them to show off the view. "Look at that lighthouse there – as white as the clouds! And see the islands turning green for the spring? Just imagine the ships that used to sail to Safe Haven. They carried silks and teas all the way from China."

In the distance, a ferry cruised home from one of the islands. Close to the rocks, a lobsterman maneuvered a red boat near a red buoy. Three seagulls swooped up on gusts of air and watched him haul a trap on board.

"Ahoy there!" Abigail put her hand on Penny's arm. "That is Mr. Cavendish, a neighbor of ours. I expect you will see him every morning."

Penny shrugged Abigail's hand off and headed further down the path. She hated being touched.

Abigail's shoulders dropped as she went after her, but John held back to watch Mr. Cavendish haul another lobster pot on board. "Good-bye!" John shouted.

Mr. Cavendish waved a lobster back at him.

John ran after Penny. "We could call him the Lobster Pirate," he said.

Penny frowned at him. She wasn't in the mood to pretend about pirates, especially with Abigail behind them.

"You never know," Abigail said. "Mr. Cavendish would probably be the best pirate in all of Beckon Bay. I have heard that he can tell stories of the ships that have sunk in the water here. The rocks go after boats when there's fog, he says."

Penny pulled John away from Abigail. "Come on," she said.

The path wove between bushes of beach roses getting ready to blossom. Then it curled away from the ocean towards a line of pine trees. Beyond them ran a long yard, ragged and vacant except for the flag flapping against a flagpole. The low concrete building behind it could only be a school.

"You found it," Abigail said as she stopped to catch her breath. "The walk is not too long, is it, Penelope Rose? You should be able to manage it in fifteen or twenty minutes."

Penny ignored her. Her stomach churned the more she thought about having to go to school. John took

23

her hand. He thought that the last school had been bad enough and now they had to start over. The idea made his head ache.

One First Day of School

Abigail led them past the school flagpole and through the heavy metal doors. "We will find John Tomas's teacher first," she said.

John began to have trouble moving his feet. Inside, the school looked the same as their last school, with fluorescent lights beating down on faded art projects. The school even smelled the same: of old milk, crayons and toilet cleaners. John walked more and more slowly. They passed several open doors before they saw a stiff old woman pinning writing samples outside a classroom.

Abigail smiled at her and took John's hand. "Here we are," she said. "John Tomas, I would like you to meet your teacher, Mrs. Sok."

"Welcome, John." John didn't say anything back, not even when Mrs. Sok asked him how old he was. Near the ocean, he could think of a million things to say. At school he forgot them all. Mrs. Sok had a face hung like wet laundry, and her hand wrung his shoulder when she used him to hobble into the classroom. She would probably want him to ask permission to yawn, he thought. Maybe she would sock students who were bad.

"We'll start today with a reading circle," Mrs. Sok told John as a crowd of boys jostled their way into the room. "Take off your hat, Watt, and throw the gum away. You should do better at showing your new neighbor how we act at school."

Abigail found Penny's classroom down the hall. Inside, a paunchy, bald man filled the chalkboard with multiplication problems. "Mr. Keenes," Abigail said, "this is Penelope Rose."

Mr. Keenes kept writing. "She's the one who wants to start school two months before vacation."

"She is the one ready for a new start." Abigail smiled at Penny.

Mr. Keenes glanced over his shoulder. He noticed Penny's faded clothes and dirty sneakers. He wasn't impressed.

Penny wasn't either. "You have cereal in your tie," she told him.

"That's poor manners." Mr. Keenes returned to the board. "You'll fit right in."

Penny glared at his back, but Abigail patted her arm. "See, Penelope Rose, you will be just like the other children." Abigail turned around, and walked into kids pushing their way into the classroom. "Oops!" Penny could hear her say in the hall. "Oops! Pardon me!"

Several of the kids laughed. "What a reject," a boy said.

Mr. Keenes grunted and stood back to count the problems on the board.

Penny kicked back a chair and slouched down in it. Just as she was getting comfortable, a girl put her hand on the desk.

"You're in my seat," the girl said.

Penny eyed her. The girl smelled like bubble gum and wore an outfit to match.

"Move," the girl said. "My stuff is in there."

Penny opened the lid to the desk so that the girl had to lift her hand. Inside the desk lay sparkly pink pencils covered in hearts. Heart-shaped erasers sat on top of a big red notebook decorated like a Valentine. "Caitlin's notebook," it declared in pink-flowered stickers. Slowly, Penny closed the desk and folded her hands on top. "So?" Penny said.

"Mr. Keenes," Caitlin said, "the new girl is in my seat."

"Mr. Keenes, it's not fair," protested a girl to her left.

"Mr. Keenes, it's not right," complained a girl in front.

Mr. Keenes reached for a doughnut on his desk. "Now, now," he said. He contemplated the board and made a problem harder.

"Make her move, Mr. Keenes," said Caitlin.

Mr. Keenes took a bite of his doughnut. "Um," he said, his cheek bulging. He took a sip of coffee. "Now, now."

"Mr. Keenes —"

"Mr. Keenes —"

Penny stood up. "Fine," she said, stalking to the back of the room. Penny found a wooden desk so beaten up that it couldn't be someone's seat. Throwing herself into it, Penny stared up at Mr. Keenes.

He ignored her. "Time for attendance, Tony," Mr. Keenes said with another sip of coffee. "Caitlin, if you please."

Caitlin flounced to the front of the room and read the lunch menu. As he stood up to count heads, Tony threw a crumpled piece of paper at Penny.

Mr. Keenes pretended not to notice. "Homework out," he said.

Penny opened the paper. "Beware," the note said. Tony had drawn a skull on the bottom, but not very well. Penny could do better with her toes. Making sure everyone heard, she tore the paper into tiny pieces. On her way to the trashcan, she kicked Tony's desk so that his papers fell across the aisle.

"Now, now," said Mr. Keenes. "None of that, new girl."

Caitlin and her friends giggled.

Penny hated school.

John didn't see Penny all morning. He sat at his desk and listened to Mrs. Sok talk about a book the class had just finished reading. In art, he drew a picture of his mother before she was sick and in social studies, he looked at a news magazine. He never said a word, not once. Mrs. Sok told him that he and Penny would have lunch at the same time, but even then he didn't talk. The other kids in his class thought he was strange and at recess, they told him so.

"Why don't you say something?" a freckled girl asked.

"You aren't stupid, are you?" asked a boy in the glasses. "Can – you – say – some – thing?"

"This kid here can't talk to you, Hank." Another boy stepped up and pushed his crooked nose into John's face. "This kid lives on Postman's Hack Road. Katie, you know the house, the one up on the cliff. He lives there with the witch. The witch cut out his tongue for dinner."

28

"No way!" Hank adjusted his glasses. "Seriously, Watt? The witch cut out his tongue?"

"She ate it with gravy," Watt said. "Toenail gravy. I saw her myself."

"Ew!" Katie jumped back. "Gross!"

John scowled. "She did not," he said.

"He talked! The new boy talked!" Katie ran to tell Mrs. Sok.

Watt looked disgusted. "If she hasn't cut you tongue out yet, she'll do it soon. Witches need protein for flying on their broomsticks."

"She's not a witch," John said.

"Yeah?" Watt knocked John's shoulder. "Why does she live in that run-down place on Postman's Hack? That's where the postman's wagon fell over the rocks. You can hear him howl when the wind blows. Everyone knows that house is haunted."

"She has the wickedest cat," Hank added. "He chews on squirrels."

"He does not," John said.

"Does too." Watt shoved him again. "I've seen him crunching on the bones."

"He does not." John shoved him back.

"Does too." Watt knocked John so hard that they both fell on the ground. Just as he was about to swing a fist, Watt saw Mrs. Sok coming. He jumped up and brushed off his pants. "You'll see," Watt said, pulling Hank away before they got into trouble. "You'll see that I'm right – right after the witch goes to take out your tongue."

One Plan

At lunch, John didn't notice that all of the kids left him to sit alone at a table. He pushed aside the slices of peaches Abigail had wrapped up in salami. He thought about the bedroom that had transformed overnight and the kitchen that had cleaned itself. It wasn't that he thought the boys were right about Abigail being a witch. He just wanted to check with Penny to see what she thought. Abigail's hair was scraggly, the way a witch's hair would be. Abigail wore striped stockings, just like witches in cartoons. John stared at his peanut butter, parsley and jelly sandwich and wondered. Abigail couldn't be a witch.

Penny tossed her lunch bag beside John's. "This school stinks," she said.

John leaned forward so nobody could hear him. "You know what the kids said at recess?"

"You should have heard what they said to me." Penny made a face. "This one girl, Caitlin, she spent all morning whispering things about Mom. But I got her back. I made a picture of what I'd do to her if she starts with me again. She gave it to the teacher, but after that, she backed off." Penny opened up her lunch bag, took one look, and closed it again. "So what did they say to you?"

"They said Abigail's a witch. They said the house was haunted and Abigail was a witch and she flies."

"That's dumb. You know that there aren't really witches."

"But she was green this morning. You even said it. That's like a witch."

Penny gestured at John's sandwich. "We'll be green, too, if we eat her lunches."

"And the room, how she'd do that so fast?"

Penny frowned. She still was asking herself that question, too.

John caught sight of Watt and Hank clearing their trays. Watt crossed his eyes and wiggled his tongue, but he stopped when Penny turned around. "The school's made up of idiots," she said.

John picked at his sandwich. "What if Abigail turned us into frogs? Or tried to cook us for dinner?"

"Now you're being stupid," Penny said, but not as if she meant it. She noticed that John had his teeth clenched the way he did whenever he was trying to be brave. He bounced his foot on the floor as if he were wishing they could run away. Penny frowned. "You know it doesn't make sense. Abigail can't be a witch."

"How do you know?"

"For one thing, why would she go to the trouble of fixing up our room if she were going to do something bad?"

"Maybe she's waiting for us to get fat."

"Not on peanut butter and parsley sandwiches." Penny got to her feet as her class began to line up. "I don't know how, but I'll prove it to you. There's no way Abigail could be a witch. You have nothing to worry about."

One Bit of Research

But John didn't think Penny was right about Abigail. Back in his classroom, he thought about the house on Postman's Hack. The wind had howled the day before, just the way Watt said. And Abigail had a black cat. Didn't all witches have black cats? John couldn't pay attention during the math groups and he didn't even bother playing with a magnet during science. On the way to the music room, John trailed behind the rest of his class. Then someone grabbed him out of line.

"Hey," he said.

"I've been watching for you," Penny told him. "I've been in the library for an hour. One of the boys kept hitting me with a ball at gym, but when I lobbed one back, they sent me to the principal. I came here instead. There's a whole bookshelf on witches."

John looked around. The library was hushed without any lights on. "Aren't we going to get in trouble?"

Penny made a face. "You'd think they'd want us to be reading." She handed him a stack of books. "These are picture books for Halloween and a lot of books on fairy tales. I don't know if they're any good, since they're supposed to be make-believe, but see if you get any ideas. I'll stick with the history books. I'll bet we find ways to prove Abigail isn't a witch."

John started with a story about a shoemaker. "Maybe Abigail is an elf. Elves are tall and skinny."

"She's not taller than most people. And in that book, elves and fairies live in flowers. So you can't believe everything you read."

"Dwarves are short," John said, opening to another story. "And brownies. Brownies do nice things and get mad when people thank them. And goblins try to take kids."

"Whatever Abigail is, she can't be a goblin. Look at how fat they are." Penny returned to her own book. "Then again, she's ugly enough."

John picked up a new book and read a few pages. "Do you think witches really hate carrots? It says here that carrots make them burp."

32

"This book says that witches have pets that help them do spells."

John pushed his book away. "Squint's a cat and he's black. Don't witches have black cats?"

"Witches probably like their pets. Abigail hates Squint." Penny looked back down at her book. "On this page, it says that witches float on water."

"I thought water made witches melt."

"This history book says that they used to throw people into big tubs of water. If they floated, everyone thought they were witches."

"If they didn't float, wouldn't they drown?"

"I guess so." Penny returned the book to the pile. "It sounds dumb to me. We can float and we're not witches."

"We can swim. Mom taught us before she got sick," John remembered. His mother had held him until he could swim on his own.

Penny remembered, too. In a bathing suit back then, their mother had looked thin and weak, but Penny hadn't understood why, not until later. Penny shook the memory away and said, "Before you got here, I read that you can tell a witch by her hands. Witches are supposed to have ugly hands."

"I don't think Abigail's hands are ugly. But her fingers are really long."

Penny began to flip through more pages. "Here it says witches have super hearing. They can hear anything from miles away."

"Abigail heard what you said about dogs, even though she was outside with the Hairy Boar." John held up his book for Penny to see. "This one's talking about potions – see? Witches drink them."

"I could see Abigail making potions. She'd probably think it was normal to mix frog's legs and cider and toothpaste and milk."

In the hall, someone called for John Tomas.

"It's Abigail." John stood up.

Penny checked the clock. "She's early."

John glanced over his shoulder. "What are we going to do? We didn't find anything out."

Penny shrugged. "So we give her carrots."

"And cider?"

"With toothpaste."

"And milk."

"All at the same time."

"And see if she burps!" John almost grinned, but then the library door bounced against the wall. He pushed the books onto a chair and sat on them. Penny rolled her eyes.

"Penelope Rose? John Tomas, there you are." Abigail held the door open for a stiff martinet of a woman. "You see, I was certain they were reading."

"Yeah, well," Penny said. "We're all for education."

"So it appears." The woman stood as tall as Abigail, with iron-colored hair and iron-rod posture. "I expected you in my office, Penny."

Abigail tried smiling. "This is Mrs. Lafontaine, Penelope Rose. Your new principal."

Mrs. LaFontaine's voice was steely and cold. "Mr. Keenes wanted me to meet you an hour ago, Penny. I had hoped we could talk over what happened in gym class."

"I already wrote an apology." Penny took a crumpled piece of paper from her pocket.

"But you were asked to deliver it to my office, weren't you? I had hoped we could talk."

"Whatever," Penny said.

Mrs. LaFontaine raised a nail-thin eyebrow. "Be aware, Penny, that Mrs. Collins has provided me with your school record. You are starting over here and we are glad to have you. But we do not tolerate any rule-breaking. I will expect you to spend recess in my office on Monday. Do you understand?"

"Yes."

Mrs. LaFontaine turned to John. "Your class missed you in the music room. Several of the boys thought you had been kidnapped." Mrs. LaFontaine's glanced melted slightly and she patted his shoulder. "Mrs. Sok will understand that you wanted to be with your sister. But in the future, you must remain with your group. No more absences from music class. Do you understand?"

John nodded.

"That is settled then." Abigail sighed in relief. "Now we will go back for your things. Mrs. LaFontaine thinks we should begin the weekend early."

"I imagine that you three need to become better acquainted," Mrs. LaFontaine said. "Take some time to figure out this new family of yours. And on Monday, Penny, you can write me an essay on what you found out."

"Great," Penny said, but it was clear she didn't mean it.

One Witch Test

"I hope you had enjoyed school today," Abigail told Penny and John as they followed the path through the shade of the circle of pine trees. "Did you have enough to eat? My books advised me to pack you a thermos of soup, but I forgot. This morning, I did not feel well. Perhaps you noticed. I felt a little green, if you can believe that."

Penny and John looked at each other behind Abigail's back.

"I am much better now." Abigail raised her arms and breathed deeply. "How could I not be? Look up, Penelope Rose, and feel that sunshine. Have you ever seen such a beautiful day?"

The ocean looked even bluer than it had that morning. Cormorants sunned themselves with their wings open wide. Sailboats bounced over the water. They seemed glad school was over, too. Penny ducked around a sumac tree and adjusted her backpack higher on her shoulders. She wouldn't have to worry about school for two whole days.

John decided to stop worrying, too. If Abigail had been sick, that would be reason enough for her to look green. As the path opened up to the ocean, he saw Mr.

Cavendish working at another buoy. Mr. Cavendish looked up and waved.

"Hello!" Abigail called. She shaded her eyes to watch as he pulled a rope tied to the blue buoy. "Did you catch anything?"

Mr. Cavendish reached over the side of his boat and dragged the square wooden crate on board. Three seagulls cried and chased one another to have the best look. Penny and John squinted, but they couldn't see if he had caught anything. Mr. Cavendish bent over for a moment before he dropped something over the side. The seagulls swept down to the surface of the water and called back to him.

"Female," Mr. Cavendish shouted. "Lot of eggs on that one." He poked fresh bait into the trap and pushed it the back into the water.

The seagulls soared up and swung down to sit on the roof of the boat's cabin.

"Better luck tomorrow," Abigail called out to him. He waved back and returned to the cockpit.

John turned to Penny. "Why couldn't he keep a female?" he asked her.

"I guess so that they'll keep making baby lobsters."

Abigail beamed. "I love that you ask questions about what you see out here. Did you know seals sometimes swim to the islands?"

It sounded like school. Penny started walking again.

"I thought you could spend the afternoon exploring," Abigail continued. "All my books talk about children playing in fresh air. Just think what you can see in the tide pools here. Perhaps you will find some of Mr. Cavendish's pirate treasure."

John noticed a piece of driftwood shaped like a sword. He swung it around the way a pirate would, but

Penny held his hand before he hit her. "Stop playing," she said. "There weren't real pirates here."

"You don't know." But John tossed his stick out into a tide pool.

"You don't know either."

"Of course," Abigail said, "my books also talk about homework. They say it is best if you do homework first thing out of school."

"No." Penny halted under the pine trees at the edge of the garden. "Your books must be wrong. We aren't supposed to do homework on Fridays. They just give it to us in case we get bored."

"Really?" Abigail wrinkled her forehead. "I was certain you were supposed to go over your lessons for Monday. But you may spend the rest of the afternoon outside while I check." She picked up a piece of paper that had just blown against her leg. "You do not have to study for a math quiz, do you? This looks as if someone lost a review worksheet."

Startled, Penny fled to the kitchen to check her backpack.

"Mrrow." Squint emerged from the tall grass in the garden. He arched his back and hissed at Abigail.

"Worry about yourself, cat." She shooed him up the back steps. "You will get fleas again if you keep sleeping outside."

Squint spat, but Abigail paid him no attention. "I have cookies for an afternoon snack," she told John, "cookies and apples and milk. My books said that cookies and milk are most popular among children, but an apple a day makes you healthy, wealthy and wise."

"That's not how it goes," John said, but he was starting to wonder about Abigail again. From the garden, he had a better view of the house than he'd had before. Broken windows on the top floors hung like sharp, gaping teeth. Something white appeared in a window and disappeared. The wind around the pine trees did make a sort of wailing sound, as if the house really were haunted. And Abigail's face was tinged with green again.

"I seem to be mixing everything up." Abigail opened the back door for him. "Perhaps you can explain over cookies and milk."

But inside the kitchen, Penny held out a baking sheet with smoking, black circles on it. "The cookies burned," she said, tossing the pan on the table.

The oven made a noise like a cough and more cookies shot across the floor.

Squint darted past John's feet to investigate. Abigail's shoulders dropped. "All my books talk about warm cookies and milk. I thought these would be ready by the time we got home."

"The oven was too hot," Penny told her. "And it's dumb to leave things cooking when you go away. You could have burned the house down. A place like this would be gone in a second."

"Oh." Abigail sank into a chair. "I am terribly sorry. And I spent all morning cooking, too." She gestured faintly at a bowl on the counter. Her hands looked bony and pale. "Would you like an apple instead?"

"It's ok," John said. He would have felt sorry for her if he hadn't started to worry again.

Penny glanced at him. "You know what I'd really like," she said, "is a carrot."

"A carrot?"

Penny nudged John. "Sure," he said.

Abigail's face lit up. "You mean a vegetable? How marvelous! All my books say that children should eat vegetables, but most children prefer not to. And carrots are so nutritious. Splendid!"

She paraded them to the refrigerator and handed them bouquets of carrots. "Each of you can fix your own carrot," Abigail said, finding a vegetable peeler in a drawer. "And now you will be helping. This will build your sense of responsibility. And if you leave the cutting for me, I will be helping, too. I think it is only fair, in light of how my cookies turned out."

Penny handed over a peeled carrot and Abigail cut it into long, smooth slices. "Thanks," Penny said innocently. "They look delicious. Would you like one?"

John watched for Abigail's reaction.

"No, thank you, Penelope Rose. You take them all. You must be hungry."

"But we need to learn how to share," Penny said. "Besides, we should start eating together. It's what families do."

Penny poked John and he nodded his head.

"Do you mean that?" Her eyes sparkled so brightly, Penny was afraid Abigail might cry. "Penelope Rose, that is the most beautiful thing you could say. We are a family now. We can celebrate with carrots. What a healthy way to begin!"

Abigail helped herself to a carrot stick and passed around the rest. They each took a bite, but nothing seemed unusual except that Abigail chewed for a long time as she ate. She chewed longer and longer, but swallowed without any kind of reaction. John looked at Penny. Penny shrugged at him. She had been right. Abigail wasn't a witch. John finished his carrot with relief.

"Heavens," Abigail said to herself. Penny and John followed her eyes to Squint on the table.

"He's smoking," John said, starting to laugh before he could help it.

Squint wasn't really smoking, but he had swallowed one of the smoking cookies. Through howls, he blew out smoke as if he'd just finished a cigar. "Yrrow!" he cried.

"He's singing," Penny began to laugh, too.

"That creature gets into more trouble than anyone I have ever met," Abigail said with her lips twitching.

"Yrrow!" Squint arched his back and coughed out a ring of smoke. He coughed out another and then toppled through the rings off the side of the table. The kitchen echoed with laughter. John held his sides, Penny held onto the counter and Abigail covered her mouth. Everyone thought they'd never seen anything so funny.

"I never have laughed this hard," Abigail gasped. "Listen to me. I think I have the hiccups —" and suddenly, she burped.

Penny and John froze.

"Pardon me," Abigail said, flushing. "How rude."

Penny and John stared at her.

Uncomfortable, Abigail picked up the rest of her carrot stick and dropped it in the trash. "I suppose somebody should help that cat," she said and went to the table.

Without a word, Penny and John went up to their room.

"She ate carrots and then she burped." Penny shut their bedroom door so Abigail wouldn't hear.

"I told you." John sat down on a bed. "She's a witch."

41

One Discovery

"We can't know for sure Abigail's a witch," Penny said. "She was laughing and hiccupping and you know what that's like. I felt like burping, too."

"But you didn't." John toyed with the stuffed poodle. "And you're not a witch."

"This doesn't prove anything. We need to do more tests. Then you'll see."

Penny found a piece of paper in one of the desks and John took a pen from a drawer. In one column, he wrote down the different tests they had found in the library. Then he drew another column. Next to the test, burp after carrots, he wrote yes.

By that night, they'd completed most of the tests. While she was bringing glasses of water to the table, Penny spilled some on Abigail and nothing happened. John wrote 'no' in the second column when they went back upstairs. After dinner, John offered Abigail a glass of apple cider and milk with toothpaste and grape jelly. Abigail drank it all. She even said he was a good cook. He wrote 'yes' in the second column. When they went for a walk on the rocks before bed, Penny slipped and pushed Abigail into a large tide pool. Abigail didn't sink, but the water wasn't that deep. John wrote 'maybe' in the second column. Abigail never showed that she knew what they were thinking, but she always heard what they said, even when they whispered. John wrote 'maybe' and 'yes' in the second column beside those tests.

"I still think she's a witch," John said as he climbed into bed. "Nobody could drink apple cider and milk together unless there was something weird about them."

Penny switched off the light. "You tried it."

"Only because you made me."

"You must be a witch then," Penny said through a yawn.

"Witches are girls."

"Not always."

"Maybe you're a witch."

"Maybe you're a freak."

"Maybe you're a long-haired, short-tailed gorilla girl."

"Shut up."

And John did.

But Penny couldn't sleep for long. When the moon was high enough to peak through the windows, she opened her eyes. Rolling over, she could see John lying on his back, with his mouth open. The breeze fanned the curtains, but outside, it was still except for the breathing of the ocean. She sat up. Something had woken her.

She slid out of bed to get a drink of water. Quietly, she crept to the door and slowly opened it into the hall. It was dark, darker than she wanted to think about. At the end of the hall, however, a light glowed under a door. At least Abigail knew that much, Penny thought. It helped if the light were on in the bathroom.

Carefully, Penny made her way forward, trying to keep the floorboards from creaking. The light grew brighter as she came closer, but something was wrong. She took another step forward. The light wasn't coming from under the bathroom door. It came from the door across the hall. It came from the door going up to Abigail's room in the attic.

Penny looked more closely. It wasn't even a normal light. Normal light, she thought, looks soft and yellow and drifts out onto a floor. But this light had glassy flecks that sparkled. And the light didn't rest calmly on the floor. Instead, it flowed back and forth, like waves on the ocean.

A hand touched her shoulder. Penny jumped and turned around. John looked at her with big eyes. "What is it?" he whispered.

Penny shook her head. "I don't know." She walked toward the light. John came even closer. Faintly, from behind the door, they heard somebody humming. Maybe if they got closer, Penny thought and took another step. The humming grew louder and outside, the pine trees sighed as the wind grew stronger.

John took Penny's hand. "Maybe we should go back to bed," he said in her ear.

"Maybe we should open the door."

John wasn't sure. As they moved closer, the light sparkled more brightly. John felt Penny's arms trembling. He wondered if she were as scared as he was. But as the wind rattled the boards on the roof, she reached for the doorknob.

The door flung itself open. The strange light fell down from dusty stairs like a waterfall, then poured onto the floor and quivered. With the light came the humming, dropping from the attic more clearly.

"Do you think it's Abigail?" John whispered.

"We should find out." Penny climbed up the first stair, then the next. John held onto her hand and followed, up and up and up, toward a round white light at the top. They climbed and climbed and all the while, the humming grew louder. Once, Penny thought she heard a word.

"Seleumbra," the voice sang.

They kept climbing. The stairs seemed to continue on forever, rising far above the house and into the sky. Still they kept climbing.

"Umbra," the voice sang high.

And suddenly at the top of the stairs, they saw the odd light leaking over the edge of an iron pot. On the pot's rim, a dark shadow fanned the green flames of a fire. Through the steam from the pot, through sparkling light, they saw the crescent of a moon through an open window. And between them and the window, between the pot and the moon, danced a figure with arms swooping.

"Penumbra. Seleumbra—"

"Mrrow," cried Squint from the pot.

"Oh," Abigail said. "Oh, dear."

Two Explanations

"You ought to be in bed," Abigail said.

Penny took a step in front of John. "You're a witch," Penny said. "You're not a real person at all."

"Of course I am a person." Abigail sounded hurt.

"Not a normal person. Normal people don't do what you're doing."

Abigail's shoulders dropped. "Oh," she said. "Probably not." She began to move through the smoke toward them.

"Stay there!" John yelled.

"Don't move!" Penny told her. "Don't you go casting any spells on us!"

Abigail hesitated and then reached out a hand to them. The steam over the pot seemed to thicken over her fingers. "You have no need to be frightened."

The steam drifted down across Abigail's dress, pooled on the floor and lapped at Penny's feet. John jumped before the steam could touch him, but he could smell cinnamon and vanilla and the damp, fishy smell of the ocean.

Penny took another step in front of John. "We know all about you," she said. "John figured it out. You're a witch. Don't lie."

"I know this looks unusual," Abigail said. "You must feel as if you were having a bad dream. Shall I bring you back to your room? You can have a good sleep and in the morning, everything will seem nice and ordinary again."

"We aren't going anywhere with you." Penny wished her voice wouldn't shake. "You might go and turn us into soup or something."

"Is that what is worrying you?" As Abigail came around the side of the pot, both Penny and John backed against the wall. Abigail stopped in surprise. "Do you really believe I am a witch like the witches in fairy tales?"

"We know what you are," Penny said.

"You do not," Abigail said. "You said I am not a person, when I am most definitely a person. And you said I would turn you into soup, when I certainly would not." She made a face and shivered. "No, absolutely not."

"But you're a witch." Penny clutched John's hand so tightly he thought she'd crush his fingers.

Abigail brushed that aside. "Technically, by your definitions, I suppose I am. But you have no need to worry. You are not in any danger."

Penny wasn't so sure. The light soaked into the floor. The wind howled over the roof and in an instant the moon vanished behind a cloud. John moved closer to his sister.

"What if I try to explain – if I tell you something secret – would you believe me then? That means something, I hope. I would be putting all my faith in you." Abigail hesitated. "Would you like to sit down?"

"We'll stand."

"Are you sure? You might be more comfortable –"

Penny glared at her.

"You will find this difficult to comprehend." Abigail took a deep breath, "The secret – the secret I share with Squint – is that we come from a someplace else. Not Maine or Boston or anywhere either of you would know. We come from a place that nobody has ever heard of. Someplace you would call magical."

"Oz?" John asked before he could help himself.

"No." Abigail smiled at him. "But sort of like Oz. If you imagine fairies and trolls, you would come close to picturing what my neighbors are like. Where Squint and I are from, things such as tree nymphs are as common as … police officers. They are everywhere."

"There's no such place," Penny said.

"There is. In fact, if you look out the window, you can see its shadow."

Penny and John peered out the window and stood back again.

"There's nothing there," Penny said. "Just clouds."

"What?" Abigail turned around. "Oh –" She closed her eyes and took a deep breath. Her face grew paler as the clouds slipped away. "There it is."

"The moon?" John looked at Penny.

Penny rolled her eyes. "We should have guessed you're from outer space."

"No, not the moon. And not outer space." Abigail motioned them closer to the window. "The shadow over the moon – do you see it? It is covering most of the moon except for that lovely crescent. Can you see?"

John nodded.

"That fuzzy black shadow is Seleumbra." Abigail said.

Two Mistakes

"Seleumbra?" John asked. "That's where you're from?"

"It is a pretty name." Abigail's eyes grew dreamy. "It always makes me think of dreaming."

"I think it's dumb," Penny said. "It all sounds dumb – and wrong. We learned about it in school. That shadow is there because the Earth is blocking sunlight from hitting the moon. There's not a Seleumbra or whatever you call it. There's no such thing."

"There is such a thing." Abigail stopped herself. Firelight flickered across her face so they could see her thinking. She thought for a long time. Finally, she said, "You see out there – the way Seleumbra lies between the Earth and the moon? I think we were, at one point, a part of Earth. But once, a long time ago, we broke away to hide in that shadow you learned about in school, Penelope Rose. Of course, since Seleumbra is hiding, no one here can see it. But they would be interested to know that we have a lot in common."

"Like what?" John asked.

"Like trees," Abigail answered. "And rocks. In fact, if you were to go to Umbra, which is where I am from, you would see how much it resembles the darkest parts of a Maine forest. When I get homesick, I like to sit beneath a pine tree on a hot day. The warm smell of fir trees, that is what the air smells like at home."

"I still don't get it," Penny said. "So you come from a magical place up in the sky. If it was so nice, why did you come here?"

"That is why we wanted you," Abigail said. "Squint and I did not come here on purpose. We were banished. Because of one mistake, we were sent away."

"That figures," Penny said. "Can't you do anything right?"

"Yes – no." Abigail stopped herself. "That is, I never intended to do anything. See there – in the sharper parts of the shadow – that is where the Umbrans live. We live alongside fairies and ogres, even if it means having to make some compromises. Pixies will steal spoons if we leave a window open, but they dance in the garden, and that is lovely.

"The people from Penumbra, on the other hand, do not want to have to lock up their spoons or fight off trolls when they want opals. In their minds, Penumbrans are superior to anybody else. They do what they want to do and the rest of us have to keep out of their way."

Penny sat down on a trunk. "So?" she asked.

"So the Penumbrans began to dictate everything. They said that mirages have to appear at set times at certain spots. An entire colony of water sprites needed to move in order for the Penumbrans to cultivate lily pads. The Penumbrans tried to control everything."

"And you did something without asking permission."

"I tried to stay out of their way," Abigail said. "It was a buccaneer who got mixed up with them – the buccaneer Zecharias Murdock Boreas Finn."

"Yrrow," said Squint at John's feet.

"Yes, yes, One-Eyed Zach. He sailed with other buccaneers in the north. Compared with the pirates in the south, the buccaneers were relatively harmless. But One-Eyed Zach was the exception. He was unusually foolish, and that made him dangerous."

Squint spat at her.

"He was foolish," Abigail repeated. "He heard that the Penumbrans wanted to tear up the ocean floor to find gold glass for their palaces. But One-Eyed Zach knew that the sea monsters would be furious if the Penumbrans damaged their ocean caves. He warned everyone that one angry sea monster could destroy every town on the coastline. He thought the Penumbrans would listen. Of course they did not. They wanted gold glass. They dug up the ocean floor searching for it."

"What happened?" John asked.

"Exactly what One-Eyed Zach had predicted. The Penumbrans disrupted a nest of sea monsters. The sea monsters became so angry that they created a tsunami. The waves swept over most of Penumbra and destroyed almost everything."

"And One-Eyed Zach?" Even if she didn't believe Abigail, Penny liked the idea of a buccaneer who knew about sea monsters.

"One-Eyed Zach was fine with sea monsters and tsunamis. He sailed his ship around rescuing Penumbrans who had been swept into the sea. As they dried off, he reminded them what he had said. He had warned them about the sea monsters."

Squint protested, but Abigail cut him off. "Yes, they should have listened. But One-Eyed Zach was foolish. He expected a reward – maybe a gold glass castle where people would tell him how smart he was. But everyone knows that Penumbrans never admit when they are wrong. We had to hold a council to discuss what had happened, and the Penumbrans could not admit a mistake, especially not with Umbrans present. They decided to blame someone else for the tsunami. The sea monsters were too frightening, so the

51

Penumbrans chose One-Eyed Zach. They said the tsunami was his fault. They said the council had to banish him as punishment."

"That's not fair," John said. "He warned them. He was right. They shouldn't have sent him away."

"That is how most of your magical creatures have come here," Abigail said. "They have all been banished here for one reason or another. Sometimes they stay. On very rare occasions, witches and fairies and centaurs and things manage to return home."

"But you? And Squint?" Penny shook her head. "I don't see how this story relates to you at all."

"The Penumbrans were so angry that they wanted to be sure One-Eyed Zach could never return home. The council could not remove his powers, not easily, that is. But it was fairly easy to transform him into something ordinary. An ordinary creature could never have the power to return to Seleumbra. So they decided to turn him into a cat."

Penny and John looked down at Squint. They looked up at Abigail. They looked down at Squint again. John rubbed his eyes.

"That's a buccaneer?" Penny asked.

"That's mean," John said.

"That's crazy," Penny said.

"Mrrow," said Squint.

"I thought it was crazy, too," Abigail said. "I do not have a high opinion of buccaneers, but even an arrogant buccaneer like One-Eyed Zach did not deserve to be banished, much less transformed. The Penumbrans were going too far. So I acted as foolishly as One-Eyed Zach. I stood up during the council to protest. Instead of stopping, they banished me, too."

Penny and John thought for a moment. John rubbed his eyes again. "They sent you here just because you tried to help One-Eyed Zach?"

"He's an ugly cat," Penny said. "And you don't even like him. I don't know why you bothered."

"Yrrow," Squint said.

"I sometimes wonder that myself." Abigail looked up through the window. The moon had moved behind pine trees and the sky had grown paler. Most of the stars had disappeared. "I miss Umbra. I would give anything to be back in my cottage. But what the Penumbrans did – what the council did – it was wrong. I had no choice. I had to try to help."

John yawned loudly before he could help it. Penny poked him, but Abigail had already become more brisk.

"And at this point of the story," Abigail said, "it is time for you to return to bed. You need to think about what I have said before I say any more. Besides, all my books say that children should never be permitted to stay up past midnight, and here it is, practically morning. Can you find your way downstairs while I finish here?"

Penny shook her head, even though it was beginning to feel heavy and tired. "We'll stay," she said, sitting back against the wall. "You still have a lot of questions to answer."

"I do not think…" Abigail began before reconsidering. "All right. First, give me a moment." She began to sing again and with a puff, the air settled on them like a soft, damp blanket. As she sang, John leaned against Penny's shoulder. Abigail sang softly and they closed their eyes.

They were sound asleep.

Two Handshakes

Penny and John did not wake up early the next morning. They slept through the sounds of seagulls calling one another to breakfast. They missed seeing Mr. Cavendish motor away to his lobster pots. By the time John opened his eyes again in their green bedroom, the sky had become a dull, practical gray. It was no day for sunshine. It was the kind of day when work needed to be done.

"You're up," Penny said. She was sitting against a pile of pillows, but she did not look comfortable. She looked serious. "I've been thinking about what Abigail said last night."

John sat up, too. "Yeah?"

"She told us that mad, wild story. She said she's a witch and Squint's a buccaneer and they got sent here from some magical place because he was right about sea monsters and gold glass."

"I believe her," John said.

Penny pushed back the covers. "Come on then."

John wasn't sure what Penny was going to do, but he followed her down the staircase. The dust beneath their feet was soft and quiet. Still, Abigail heard them before they came into the kitchen.

"Good morning." Abigail sounded cautious.

Penny marched up to the counter. "I'm not saying we believe your story about being from outer space." She glanced at Squint, placidly licking a paw. "And even if you've got one ugly cat, it doesn't make him a buccaneer – or you a witch. It was a good bedtime story, but you left out the important part. You still never said what you're planning on doing with us."

Abigail looked over Penny's shoulder. "What do you think, John Tomas?"

John shook his head. "We can't send you back home. We don't know how."

"You know how to peel carrots and make a sandwich and arrange a bedroom." Abigail shook her head. "Even after reading a library full of books, I cannot figure out how to mix porridge properly." She held out a pot.

John wrinkled his nose. The oatmeal was black and oozing.

Penny pushed it away. "You're not answering the question."

Abigail dropped the pot into the sink. "Do you remember what I said last night – about Seleumbra being different than it is here? I do not know how to drive a car and I do not know how shop for groceries. In order to get by, I have had to manage the way I did on Seleumbra. And when I do something here that you would call magic, I have no energy for anything else. I could hardly stand after I finished decorating your bedroom that first night. Yesterday morning, I resorted to using a little magic and that finished me for the most of the day. If I keep wasting my energy on ordinary things, I will not have the strength for the trip back to Seleumbra."

"I still don't get it," Penny said.

55

"Just consider," Abigail said. "Consider how far away Seleumbra is. Squint and I will have to travel very far very quickly and that will take a great deal of magic. For months, we have tried to find a magic formula that will move us closer. For months, I have tried to store up my strength so we can use the formula once we find it. Nothing has worked. We still need the formula and I still need to be stronger. I cannot waste my powers on making oatmeal that tastes right. I need to start living without my magic powers."

"What do you want us to do?" John asked, sitting down at the table. "We don't know any magic formulas."

"But you know how to do things," Abigail said. "You could teach me how to do things without magic. Already you taught me about sandwiches. Making your school lunch yesterday was a big accomplishment for me."

"It was a lousy lunch," Penny said, "and you have cookbooks. If you read them more carefully, you'll get the idea. You don't need us to teach you."

"I need to learn more than cooking." Abigail sat down across from John. "If you wanted, you could teach me how to shop and clean – and – paint a bathroom wall."

John nodded. He and Penny had cooked and cleaned for their mother all the time.

But Penny shook her head. "Social Services did not put us here to teach you about oatmeal. You're supposed to be taking care of us."

Abigail looked up at her. "I realize I am asking you to take on more responsibility than most children can handle. But I know you could help me. When your mother was ill, you cared for her, as well as for

56

yourselves. In the worst circumstances, you managed the world much better than I have alone. You know how to do things and I have a home. It is a good match."

"And what if we said no?" Penny asked. "We could call up Social Services and tell them what you're making us do. Mrs. Collins could put us with a different foster family."

John looked at Penny. He didn't think she meant what she said. Penny wouldn't risk Mrs. Collins placing them in separate homes. John swallowed.

Abigail bit her lip. "I would understand, of course. Likely, Mrs. Collins could find you lovely foster parents. But I could help you, too. I thought about it months ago. In exchange for teaching me how to live normally, I could help you find a family."

Penny crossed her arms. "John and I are a family. We don't need anyone else."

"You may not want anyone else, but the law says that you must have an adult guardian." Abigail hesitated. "I thought I could help you find more than a guardian. I thought I could find the perfect family to adopt you."

"The perfect family?" John repeated.

Penny rolled her eyes. "Like one with a real bathroom and parents who know how to cook?"

Abigail looked hurt, but she said, "I am sure we could find someone."

"You'd better not be thinking of some other foster family with 14 kids in a trailer," Penny said. "You can't hand us off to anyone who's looking for kids in order to get a check from the government. You'd better be thinking of people who'd really want us."

"Naturally," Abigail said. "I have read all about families. They love you and you love them and everyone takes care of one another."

"They'd have to be normal people," Penny interrupted. "Like, they'd have to have a car and a TV. And a real backyard – with a dog."

"Yrrow," Squint said.

"I like cats," John put in. "They could have cats, too."

"Fine. Cats and dogs and bunnies, too, if they want. They could have a whole zoo, but they'd better be good people."

"What about a computer?" John asked Penny. "Do you think they could have a computer? With games?"

"Of course they'll have a computer. They'll have real jobs. Plus, they'll make enough money to buy whatever we need – at real stores in the mall." Penny thought for a moment. "Maybe they'll have a swimming pool."

"And a trampoline." John hugged his knees. "And we'll have so many toys, it'll be like a toy store."

"But they'll be like actual parents. The dad will show us things and the mom will take care of us. She'll be pretty and he'll be tall."

"We'll go on airplanes all the time."

"And we'll do things like ride horses."

"Like cowboys." John's face was glowing.

"Mrrow," Squint said.

Penny looked down at Abigail. "Did you get all that? It's no deal unless they're perfect."

Abigail nodded slowly. "That is my promise."

"Fine." Penny reached out her hand. Abigail took it, her long fingers locking tightly around Penny's palm. "So it's a deal. What do you want to learn first?"

Abigail took a deep breath. "I have no idea. Where should we start?"

"Breakfast," John suggested. "I'm hungry."

"Breakfast it is." Abigail tried to smile.

"Mrrow," Squint said.

Two Different Worlds

John told Abigail everything he knew about cereal while Penny poured glasses of juice. He opened the cupboard and showed Abigail how to recognize healthier cereals by their plain-colored boxes. He taught her how to read the boxes to find out about the vitamins and then how to open the tops carefully so they could close again.

"That is just the sort of lesson I had hoped you would give me," Abigail said as he poured cereal in a normal-sized bowl. "Perhaps tomorrow, you can teach me about toast."

"Or French toast," John said. "I like French toast. Penny makes yummy French toast."

"That sounds good." Abigail looked to Penny. "Could you teach me that, too?"

Penny shrugged. "Cooking isn't so important. We can cook until you learn how. You should focus on bigger things."

"Right," Abigail said. "What is the biggest thing?"

Penny considered. "The house is pretty bad. John and I need to take baths and do laundry. And you should get groceries. You must have used up a whole carton of eggs yesterday at breakfast."

"I did," Abigail said proudly. "And my books say a kitchen should always have eggs. I propose that we start with shopping. You can show me what we need in order to scrub out the bathroom."

After she and John finished their cereal, Penny searched through the cupboards to see what supplies Abigail already had. In the meantime, John showed Abigail how to wash dishes. "It's ok if you get wet?" he asked as Abigail reached into the drain after a turnip top.

"Of course. But your water is not very pleasant. Our water feels thicker. If you fell into our ocean, you would float right to the surface."

"So everyone can swim?"

"Everyone can swim on the surface. Seals, for instance, paddle along in the sunshine. If Squint wanted a seal to tell his fortune, he would just lean over the bow of his boat and ask."

Squint tried to interrupt from his seat on the stove, but Abigail talked over him. "Yes, yes, sea monsters and mermaids can swim down to the ocean floor. Did I not tell them about the sea monsters last night?"

Squint began to argue back, but John was too excited to listen. "You have mermaids? And seals? Regular seals like ours?"

Penny stuck her head around the pantry doorway. "How can they be regular seals if they can tell fortunes?" She looked down at the puddle growing below the sink. "You don't have a mop, do you?"

"No," Abigail said. "But there should be a broom here somewhere."

John dropped his sponge. "For flying?"

"For cleaning." Abigail laughed as John's face fell. "I needed to sweep out your room before I put down the new rugs."

"And she can't go flying anyway," Penny cut in. "Not if she's trying to act like a regular person. Regular people don't fly on broomsticks."

"Very true." Abigail turned off the faucet and wiped her hands on her skirt. "So there will be no flying today, if you do not mind, John Tomas. But we could take the bus into town to go to one of the large supermarkets. Or if you would rather, we could walk to Mal's Market. It is just beyond your school."

"It'll be faster if we walk," Penny said, "but we need a lot of cleaning supplies – and milk. It'll be a lot to carry."

"I think we can manage. Go brush your teeth while I find my scarf. All my books say dental hygiene is essential."

"I think it would be awesome if we could fly," John said to Penny as he rinsed his toothbrush.

"Knowing Abigail, we'd crash into a building." Penny spat into the sink, but the sink spat back. "We're going to need a plumber," she said.

The toilet gulped. The bathroom light flickered and died.

"And an electrician," John said.

The bulb over their head popped.

Two Clues

They had nearly as much work to do outside as they did inside on the house. Penny noticed how splintered and broken the wood was on the back steps. She noticed how shaggy and unkempt the grass looked in the backyard. The stone wall between the pine trees had crumbled into rubble. An old wire drooped and fell

61

short of the house. They should get a new clothesline, too, she thought.

Abigail came beside her and took a deep breath. "We are going to have an adventure today. Can you smell it in the air, John Tomas?"

John tried. He smelled salt and fish and damp. There was no warmth in the air and there were heavy clouds in the sky. "I think it's going to rain."

Abigail took his hand as they followed Penny to the stone path. Squint darted ahead, but Abigail stopped at the wall to look out at the ocean. Today, gray and hushed, it hardly seemed to move. "You know, this is the most time I have spent near the ocean," Abigail said. "Squint sailed on Seleumbra, but where I grew up, it was all forest and hills. But deep in my mountains, you can find emeralds – and dragons."

"Real dragons?"

"Great big green ones and little baby blue ones."

John thought about dragons. He thought about mermaids and seals that told fortunes. He thought about gold glass and buccaneers and sea monsters and he laughed. He laughed and laughed and ran ahead to Penny. "I'm going to be a buccaneer," he announced. "I am going to go sailing every day."

Penny stepped off the path onto a boulder. "You're going to have to do a lot of the cleaning if I have to do the cooking. It won't give you a lot of time to mess around with Abigail."

John didn't care. "She used to live near dragons."

"If you say so." Penny jumped onto a boulder closer to the water. John jumped over a tide pool and onto another boulder.

"Just keep heading that way!" Abigail pointed towards the lighthouse.

Penny and John leaped from rock to rock, stopping only to look at what had been caught during high tides. Broken white clamshells filled crevices and red-striped buoys cracked in the sun. Close to the path, Penny found a smashed lobster pot that had been lost during a storm. Close to the water, John found a tide pool filled with white barnacles and blue mussels. The rocks were ridged like the bark of an oak tree. Between one of the ridges, John found a tiny bottle.

"What's that?" Penny hopped down to see.

Salt-crusted and chipped, the blue bottle was no bigger than the palm of John's hand. The stopper, though, curved just as wide and glittered brand new. Thin gold wires met and twisted to make something like an open soccer ball.

"There's a piece of paper inside the bottle." John held the bottle up to the light. "But I can't read what it says."

"Don't squish the top. It's pretty." Penny watched John struggle for a moment. The round stopper didn't move. Penny tried herself before handing the bottle back to John. "I can't get it to open either."

"Did you find something, John Tomas?" Abigail nearly tripped over her scarf in her hurry to reach him on the boulder. "Is it a note? May I see?"

Without waiting for him to answer, Abigail took the bottle. She held it upside down while a breeze whipped around her skirt and up her arms. With a pop, the stopper came into her hand. The paper slid out behind it.

"You're not supposed to be doing that anymore." Penny put her hands on her hip. "That thing you do with the wind. Your skin is turning green and everything."

"This is special." Abigail sounded like it was hard to keep her voice calm. "You cannot understand – for months, Squint and I have searched and searched. Last night in the attic, I was trying to find it – and this morning, after everything, here it is."

"What is it?" John looked over her arm.

Abigail leaned down to show him. "This, John Tomas, is the special formula, the very formula I mentioned this morning. This is the first step of our journey back to Seleumbra."

Penny tried to read the swirls and squiggles. "It doesn't make any sense."

"Someone from Seleumbra wrote it many years ago." Abigail skimmed the writing and nodded to herself. "You can read her name here – Evie was the witch who hid this formula. She figured out what she would need to get home and left it behind in case someone else would want it. Squint and I tried to find the formula in her house – our house on Postman's Hack Road. Unfortunately, we did not find anything there. We did not even see any clues. I suppose we needed you to find them, John Tomas."

"And now you don't need us anymore?" John asked.

Abigail hugged him. "Of course we do. This formula, precious as it is, requires a great deal of magic to carry out."

"So you still have to learn how to do things without magic?"

"Yes, Penelope Rose, I do. This will make things much easier, but I will still need my strength." Abigail tucked the paper inside her striped stocking. "I believe the stopper is nothing extraordinary, but the bottle is from Seleumbra. If you would like to keep them both, John Tomas, please do with my compliments."

"Really?" John examined the bottle more closely. Pressed into the blue glass were more swirls and squiggles.

"I don't see why the formula was so hard to find," Penny said as they climbed back onto the path. "That old witch should have left it somewhere obvious if she wanted to help you."

"That is what Squint and I had hoped when we first arrived here," Abigail said. "We ought have known better. Evie certainly did. She knew there are Penumbrans here – Keepers, they call them, to keep us from escaping back home. The Keepers would have destroyed her formula if they had found it. The Keepers do not want us to find a way home."

John laughed before he could help it. Witches and buccaneers – magic formulas in hidden bottles – enemy Keepers to avoid – it was all an adventure. "Hey, One-Eyed Zach!" John shouted, running down the path. "Guess what!"

"Don't stop," Penny called after him. "Keep on going. We need to get to the supermarket before it starts raining."

"You are right, Penelope Rose." Abigail pulled up her stockings up over her boots. "Enough with Seleumbra and magic formulas. It is time to start behaving normally."

Two Encounters

Squint didn't lead them up the turn they had taken to go to school. Instead, he followed the path as it wove away from the coast and to a faded supermarket. Neon letters spelled out "Mal's Market", but only the first M was lit up. The T flickered every time a car drove over the speed bumps in the parking lot.

"I have never shopped here," Abigail said. "Before you came, I made things appear from storage places or stores. In fact, I am not sure where I got all the fruit from your lunches." She shook her head. "No, from here on, I will be a model of integrity. All my books say that honor is important."

Squint made a rude noise, but Abigail pointed him to the sidewalk. "You can wait there and growl all you like. Do not scratch anyone."

John gave Squint a salute. "We'll be out soon," he said.

But Penny and John couldn't move Abigail quickly through the store. John had to spend five minutes showing her how the motion detector worked on the doors. At the deli counter, Penny had to stop her from pulling several numbers off the ticket roll.

"You're going to mess everything up," Penny whispered. "Look at how many people are waiting to give their orders. We don't need cold cuts and you've got seven different kinds of cheese in the refrigerator."

Abigail apologized. "It is my first time shopping," she explained to the clerk behind the counter.

"You mean, it's your first time shopping here." Penny apologized to the clerk and dragged Abigail away. "You can't say things like that. People are going to think you're strange if you tell them you've never done anything normal."

"I will not say another word." But her eyes lit up as she noticed a tank in the corner. "Penelope Rose, look – pet lobsters!"

"Come on." John pulled on her arm. "We can get the dish soap."

"And floor cleaner," Penny told him. "I'll get paper towels."

When John tried to choose a dish detergent, Abigail squeezed the bottles so the soap squirted across the floor. When John tried to pick a floor cleaner, Abigail pulled off the plastic wrappings to test the smells. When at last Penny said they had everything on the list, John thought Abigail's first day of shopping had gone well. Then the worst thing happened.

"$56.43," said the clerk at the cash register.

Abigail smiled at him.

John nudged her.

"You need to pay," Penny said.

Abigail's eyes widened. "Pay?"

John nodded.

"John Tomas – I did not bring any money." Abigail turned around. "Penelope Rose, I did not realize."

Thinking furiously, Penny stepped around the shopping cart. "I'm sorry," she said to the clerk. "She –

um, she must have left her wallet at home." Penny glared at Abigail. "It was really stupid. We can put everything back and come again later."

"There is no money at the house, Penelope Rose," Abigail whispered. "I could use my – "

"Be quiet," Penny broke in. "You'll make it worse."

The clerk flicked a switch so that a light flashed over the cash register. "You're going to have to talk to Mal. She's not going to be happy."

"I regret this deeply," Abigail said. "I apologize for the bother."

"Tell that to Mal," the clerk repeated. He leaned forward and said confidentially, "When Mal caught some kid shoplifting, she nearly tore his arms off. It was scary." The clerk ducked his head. "Here she is."

"Herbert Harris Parker, what is going on?" Mal demanded. She had a hoarse voice that sounded as if she spent most of her time yelling. She had arms that looked as if they spent most of their time squeezing people – or at least, squeezing people's legs. Penny didn't think Mal could reach up higher than John's shoulders. Before he could help it, John invented a name for her. Small Mal, he thought to himself.

"They can't pay," Herbert said.

"It is my fault," Abigail explained. "I had no money."

"We can put the stuff back," Penny said. "It's no big deal."

"But we need to clean the bathroom, Penelope Rose –"

"It's ok," Penny said, even though it wasn't.

Mal frowned. She put her hands on her hips and peered up at Abigail. "Have you ever been here before?"

Abigail shook her head. "It was my first time shopping. The children were helping me."

"These are your children?" Mal eyed them.

Penny was growing frustrated. "She's supposed to be our foster parent," she said, "not that it's any of your business. And it's not any of your business that she's had us for just a few days and has no clue what to do about anything. She messed up today, but we made a deal to help out and so now we want to know what you want us to do. We could put the stuff away for you. Or we could come back with money later."

"Hm." Mal thought. She glanced out the window and took a cigar out of her pocket. "How about this," she said, chewing off of the end of her cigar. "Under these special circumstances, how about we can come to an arrangement? After all, we are here to help our customers. In this special case, you can help us."

Herbert goggled at her. "You're not making them pay?"

Mal nodded at Abigail. "It sounds as if they need some leeway on their first visit."

"That is very kind of you," Abigail said hesitantly. She bit her lip.

"You may not thank me when you are through. Nobody wants to do these jobs." Mal pointed over Abigail's shoulder at John. "You, come with me."

Mal had John push their cart of groceries behind a counter. "You seem capable of wheeling carts well enough," she said, "and I have nobody collecting carts outside for me. Is that something you can handle?"

John nodded.

"Good." Mal waved Penny over. "Someone has made a mess of the floors near the detergents. Detergent is everywhere and customers are sliding all over the place. Find a mop in the back and clean it up. Afterwards, you can go behind all the counters and mop there. As for you," she said to Abigail, "you can stay up front and help with the bagging. Try to move the lines along."

"I think I can manage that," Abigail said. "How difficult could it be?"

None of the jobs were easy, though. With Squint directing him from the top baskets, John rammed the carts together and pushed them into a long line through the parking lot. But the clouds began to fall lower, bringing a heavy mist that made the cart handles slippery. John's fingers became stiff, his nose became stuffy, and before long, the mist changed into a cold, unhappy drizzle. John thought he was getting sick when he heard someone call his name.

"What on earth are you doing here, Buster?"

Penny had little trouble cleaning up the smears of detergent on the floor. But when she wheeled her mop behind the deli counter, Penny found a tub of spoiled cottage cheese that someone had forgotten to refrigerate. Behind the fish counter, Penny found a garbage bag of moldy squid that someone had forgotten to throw away. Penny knew she was going to be sick and then she heard someone snort behind her.

"Just what do you think you are doing, Missy?"

At the checkout counter, Penny and John saw Abigail in front a long line of customers. She loaded potatoes onto a loaf of bread in one bag, and whirled around to drop it in a shopping cart. She put a gallon of ice cream with a hot roasted chicken in another bag, and whirled around again. Abigail looked as if she were getting dizzy and Penny and John wondered if it would make her sick. But a snort over their shoulders made them cringe first. "Miss McKinney, what is the meaning of this?"

Abigail dropped a carton of orange juice onto a carton of eggs. Juice dribbled onto her boots, but she didn't notice. "Yes?" she asked wearily. She froze. There stood Mrs. Collins.

Mrs. Collins jerked John and Penny in front of her. "On a whim, I decided to stop in for a pack of cigarettes. To my surprise, Buster here was arranging carts in the parking lot. We found Missy carrying trash out to the dumpster. These children appear to be employees of the store, Miss McKinney, but how can that be? Children this young can't be working. It's illegal."

Abigail bit her lip.

Herbert cleared his throat. "Excuse me, ma'am," he said, "but you're in the way."

Mrs. Collins snorted. "I hope you have an explanation, Miss McKinney."

"What is going on?" Mal marched up to Mrs. Collins and jabbed her leg. "You are disrupting business."

"Are you the manager here?" Mrs. Collins shook Penny and John by their shoulders. "Did you employ these children?"

"And what if I did?" Mal jabbed her finger into Mrs. Collins' thigh. "They agreed. Their guardian, too. I do not see why you have to butt in."

"Really?" Mrs. Collins pulled Penny and John closer. "I'll have you know that I can take these children away right now. Just like that. It's my job."

"Your job?" Mal spat out a wad of cigar. "Fine. Do your job. Take them away if you think they have been mistreated."

71

"I just might."

"Mrs. Collins, please." Abigail held out a hand. "You should know that the children's behavior has been admirable over the past few days. Just this morning, they have done exemplary work here – under very trying circumstances. I think you can let them go."

"If you are not going to take them away," Mal said, "you might as well leave."

"Yeah," Herbert said.

"That's right," said a customer in line. "You're holding us up, lady."

Outside, there was a rumble of thunder.

"Fine." Mrs. Collins pushed Penny and John out of the way. "You want to put them to work? If it keeps them out of trouble, I won't argue. It's about time they made themselves useful."

"They have," Abigail said. "Come any time and you will find out how wonderful they are."

Mrs. Collins' lip curled. "We'll see." She swept her purse up to her shoulder and marched away.

"So long," Herbert called after her. He looked back at the customer. "What a witch."

Abigail smiled gratefully at Mal. "You did not have to help us like that," she told her.

"People can surprise you." Mal finished her cigar with one last bite. "You may as well go home now with your groceries. You have earned your groceries."

"We earned them this week," Penny said, gathering their bags behind the checkout counter. "I don't know what we'll do when we have to go shopping again."

"I shall get a job," Abigail said. "Ordinary people have jobs. I could work while you are at school."

"She couldn't work here, could she?" John asked Mal.

"I cannot afford to let her work again. Look at that." Mal pointed her cigar at the groceries Abigail had packed. A long glob of egg dangled through a hole in a bag.

"Bet you broke every egg in that one," Herbert said, impressed.

Mal grunted. Penny sighed.

"They're hiring at the Clam Counter across the street," the customer told them. "They have a sign up for a dishwasher."

"I can do dishes." Abigail's face shone. "I learned this morning."

Outside, the sun shone through a break in the clouds.

"At least it stopped raining," Penny said.

John sneezed.

"And I'm going to want a new carton of eggs," the customer told Mal.

Two Calamities

All the way home, Abigail had to stop herself from walking on air. Over lunch, Abigail had to be careful not to make the sandwiches fly. Afterwards, when John taught her how to scrub a bathtub clean, Abigail had to bite her lip to keep from singing songs from Seleumbra.

"I just cannot believe how well everything is progressing," Abigail said with a swipe of her sponge. "You found the formula to help us get home. You taught me all I need to know to get a job. And now you showed me how clean bathtubs!"

Penny watched the water swirl down the drain. It left a rust-colored puddle behind. "You need a plumber."

"After I get a job, we can get ten plumbers – carpenters, too, if you like." Abigail sat back on her feet and looked around proudly. "If John Tomas teaches me how to sweep the floor, we could turn this into a model bathroom easily."

"Here." John held the broom out to her, but when it knocked against the ceiling, a shower of plaster fell onto the floor. Sputtering, Penny wiped her eyes. John sneezed and wiped his nose.

Abigail looked at the specks collecting in the bathtub. "Perhaps cleaning will not be so easy," she said, picking up the sponge to start again.

Still, by the end of the weekend, even Penny was impressed by the amount Abigail had learned. When they came downstairs for breakfast Sunday morning, Abigail had set the table with the appropriate bowls and spoons. While they did their homework, Abigail washed the dishes, wiped out the sink and swept most of the dust off the floors. By Monday morning, Abigail said she was more than ready to apply for a job.

"I will go to the Clam Counter after I drop you off at school," she said as they walked down the path Monday morning. "And if you do not see me when school lets out, come by the restaurant. Perhaps I will be washing dishes already."

John had trouble concentrating at school that day. His nose was still stuffed up from working in the rain, and his head felt heavy and hot. He didn't mean to, but he kept thinking about Seleumbra. On the top of his math paper, he made up names for dragons and didn't hear the directions about coloring in shapes with right angles. In reading, he stared at his book and remembered the squiggles on his blue bottle. Watt stuck his crooked nose in John's face again when John held up the line on the way to recess. After lunch, Katie pinched him so he would look at the fire engines racing past the window. John had no trouble hearing the bell ringing at the end of school, however. He wanted the day to be over.

Penny had trouble in school that day, but it was a different sort of trouble. Whenever Mr. Keenes turned his back, Tony swung around in his seat and shot a spitball at her. Eventually, Tony aimed for the blades of

Mr. Keenes' fan, which spun so fast that they shot the spitballs back harder, right at Penny's head. If Mr. Keenes heard the giggles or if he noticed the wads of paper on the floor, he didn't seem to care. He even stepped over a large, gooey spitball as he passed out paint for their art projects.

"You don't need any art supplies," Mr. Keenes told Penny. "It's your turn to bring us the milk for snack. And don't forget – you're in the office today for recess."

"Ha-ha!" Tony said.

Caitlin and the other girls giggled.

Penny leaped to her feet. Normally, she would have hated carrying the heavy box of milk cartons back to the classroom. That day, though, she was glad to escape. She wanted to get back at Tony – at everyone – but she had to find a really good way. Penny was still plotting when she stumbled over a box of milk cartons in the hallway.

"Be careful," said one of the cooks in the cafeteria. "Don't take those. They've gone bad. A custodian is coming to throw them away."

Penny nodded, but when the cook went back to work, Penny grinned and picked up the box. She wasn't thirsty, but everyone else was.

When Penny returned to her classroom, Caitlin was collecting the paint. Other students milled around getting their snacks. Nobody noticed the expiration date as Penny left milk cartons on each desk. Tony, on the other hand, did look up when Penny passed by his desk.

"Henny-Penny," he crooned, "look here."

Penny had just enough time to see the rubber band in his hand. She dodged and the rubber band hit one of

76

the boys in the front of the room. The boy swung back and knocked into Caitlin. Caitlin stumbled. The tray of cups and paint flew into the air. They tipped and –

"Hey, watch out!"

"You got paint all over me!"

"Mr. Keenes, look what she did."

"There's paint all over my project!"

"I've got it in my hair!"

On the other side of the aisle, a boy gagged on a gulp of milk. A girl coughed up a sip. A boy sputtered milk across his desk.

"Gross."

"The milk tastes funny."

"It's chunky-"

"Mr. Keenes –"

Caitlin began to cry. "My new dress! Mr. Keenes, it's got paint on it."

"Someone spit milk on you, too." Penny sniffed. "Is that you who smells?"

"Mr. Keenes!" Caitlin wailed.

"Now, now." Mr. Keenes sighed as he turned around from the chalkboard.

Penny smiled sweetly back at Caitlin. "You've got something on your nose."

Caitlin grabbed a cup of paint. "See how you like it," she said and threw the paint across the room. Penny jumped out of the way. The paint splashed over the window, over the wall and over the whirring blades of Mr. Keene's fan. As the fan whipped around, droplets of paint spat onto the class and everywhere.

"Enough now!" Mr. Keenes finally lost his temper. He strode forward, but his foot landed on Tony's biggest, wettest spitball. Mr. Keenes slipped and with a splat, he landed into a puddle of paint on the floor. The room erupted.

Later, after the bell rang at the end of the day, Penny ran up to John and slung an arm around his shoulder. "How was school?" she asked, ruffling his hair.

He ducked under her arm and looked at the paint speckled across her face. "What happened to you?"

Penny laughed. "It was the best day ever."

"Hrrow!" Squint sprung down from the roof of a car in front of them.

Penny took a step back, but John leaned down. "What's up, Zach?" he asked.

"Hrrow!" Squint leaped ahead of them. He stopped, looking back, and flicked his tail.

"What?" Penny asked.

"I think he wants us to follow him," John said.

Squint dashed down the street.

Penny and John ran after him to the street corner. Squint, his tail twitching, gazed across the street at the place where the Clam Counter should have been. Instead of a restaurant, they saw a smoking ruin of a building. Firefighters were packing their gear away, but Abigail sat on the curb, her face streaked with soot, her purple scarf singed at the ends.

"I have to hand it to her," Mal said behind them. Leaning against the wall of her market, Mal puffed on a cigar and chuckled. "She solved one problem for me. The traffic out of the Clam Counter drove me nuts."

"Come on," Penny muttered to John and they ran across the street.

"Hello," Abigail said. "How was school?"

"What happened?" John asked.

"What did you do?" Penny said.

78

Abigail smiled faintly. "I got the job," she said. "They put me to work right away. You would have been proud."

"But there was a fire," John said.

"Apparently, they wanted one." Abigail shook her head. "All my books talked about the dangers of kitchen fires. Even Mal came by this morning to warn me against accidents in the kitchen. I had no idea that anyone might want to flame-broil a swordfish. When I saw a large flame and a full bucket on the floor, I thought it was a lucky coincidence."

"But you didn't put the fire out?" John coughed.

"It was a bucket of oil, " Abigail explained. "They said that I made the fire worse."

The roof collapsed with a swoosh of ashes.

"You think?" Penny asked.

Abigail sighed. "I have to find a new job. They said I am not safe in a kitchen."

"You aren't."

John put a hand over his eyes. His head hurt, but he tried to sound cheerful. "You made a good lunch today. I like apples in my turkey sandwich."

Abigail laughed wryly. Then she blinked. "Penelope Rose, why are you covered in green spots? No – " she shook herself. "Tell me on the way home. You both need an afternoon snack."

But when they arrived at the house, instead of a snack, they found Mrs. Collins tapping her umbrella. She took one look at them and snorted. "Just as I thought," she said.

Two Reasons To Worry

"So," Mrs. Collins said, "you told me to stop by any time. At any time, you said I would hear how wonderful your angels are. Instead, I find out that Buster, there, is falling asleep during reading lessons. Missy, on the other hand, has to spend her recess this week with the principal. She's starting paint fights, I hear. This doesn't sound like angelic behavior to me, Miss McKinney."

Penny glared at her. John tried to swallow, but his throat hurt.

Abigail bit her lip. "Would you like some tea?"

Mrs. Collins screwed up her face. "You smell like a barbecue. What have you been doing?"

Abigail tried to smile as she opened the front door. "We have had an interesting day. Please come in."

A puff of plaster fell across the doorway.

"And here's another thing." Mrs. Collins poked her umbrella at the doorway. "I overlooked your housekeeping before, but at this point, I'm done making allowances. Who knows how your ceiling stays up. And just listen to this – the porch sounds as if it will break through."

She bounced up and down so they could hear the wooden boards creak. The boards on the porch sagged lower and lower. "Clearly, this is unacceptable," Mrs. Collins said as the wobbles of her jowl flopped up and down. "This house is a disgrace."

But at that moment, all her bouncing had an effect. With a crash, Mrs. Collins fell right through the floor, right up to her flabby bottom. She screamed, Abigail screamed and Squint leaped onto the porch railing for a better view.

"Help me!" Mrs. Collins flailed her arms and wiggled, but still, she couldn't pull herself out of the porch. She whacked Penny in the jaw when Penny tried to come closer and she socked John in the stomach when he tried to reach her hand. Finally, Abigail grabbed hold of her arms and yanked her out of the hole.

"Did you hurt yourself?" Abigail patted her down frantically, but Mrs. Collins pushed her away. A light bulb over the door exploded with a spray of sparks. Dust rained down on them from the porch ceiling. Beneath their feet, the boards groaned again.

Mrs. Collins jabbed a finger at Penny. "I can take you right now," she said. "There's a space for you at that girl's home, ready and waiting. And I've found a family for your brother, too. Sixteen boys – he'll fit right in."

"No," Penny said. She felt icy cold and reached out for John's hand. "No, you can't separate us."

"That's not for you to decide." Mrs. Collins adjusted her underwear. "There are rules about these things. I'm supposed to see that you live someplace safe and clean."

"This is safe," Penny said. John coughed and she added, "We can make it cleaner."

"You will see improvements before the week is out," Abigail said. "I give you my word."

Mrs. Collins grunted. "I suppose it'll take that long to get the paperwork done." She brushed off her jacket and stared at Penny and John. They stepped closer together.

"Fine," Mrs. Collins said, "I'll give you the week. But this is your last chance to prove to me that you –" she pointed at Abigail, "can raise these children without

81

the house falling to pieces. And you two –” she pointed at Penny and John, “need to prove that you can behave in a classroom. You have four days.”

She tripped over Squint nibbling at a cobweb, and then limped down the walk to her car. The gate swung shut behind her. With a roar, her car drove away.

Two Ways To Go

“Well,” Abigail said after a moment. “Yes. Well.”
John sneezed.
Penny looked at him. His nose was pink and his legs trembled. John was sick and she hadn’t realized. Penny was supposed to make sure they stayed together, but at school, she had forgotten to be careful. Penny tried to swallow, but her throat had become hard.

“Come now.” Abigail shook herself. “We will be fine. Shall we make a pie? In my books, pies always sound cozy and filling.”

John sniffled and coughed. He felt hot and cold at the same time.

Penny blinked furiously. Abigail didn’t know how to make a pie. Abigail didn’t know how to clean her house. Abigail didn’t know how to do anything that would prove that they should stay together. Penny’s eyes burned.

“Before we start the pie, we should get cleaned up,” Abigail said. “John Tomas, you look like you need a tonic. Is your head bothering you? I really ought to look after you better.”

Abigail didn’t know how to look after John, Penny thought, wiping her eyes roughly. It was Penny who needed to figure out what to do. She shook her head to clear her eyes, but it didn’t help. She had to get out –

she had to think. Penny stumbled over Squint and the hole in the floor. Penny ran, back around the house towards the ocean.

"Penelope Rose? Where are you going?" Abigail called after her.

But Penny didn't stop. She cut through the grass. She tripped over the stone wall and let the wind blow her along the ocean path. She didn't head to the school or Mal's Market. This time, she ran the opposite direction.

"Penelope Rose!" Abigail turned to John. "I do not understand. Is she running away?"

John slouched against the door. "No."

"I should go after her." But Abigail stopped when John started coughing. "And you are not well either." She hesitated and said, "Squint – Zach, please, would you see that Penelope Rose is alright?"

"Mrrow," Squint said, pausing to stretch.

Abigail pushed him towards the steps with her foot. "Go on, you useless creature. Make sure she comes back safely."

"Hrrow," said Squint as he sauntered away.

Abigail watched the cat disappear into the weeds in the garden. "What a terrible mess I have made of things, John Tomas. I am so sorry."

"Penny'll be ok." The world tilted and John leaned against her arm. He felt very tired. "It was the same at the hospital. When it got really hard. But she came back."

Abigail squeezed his hand. "Is it still hard?"

John took a deep breath, but it hurt. "Yeah."

Abigail thought for a moment. "I suppose we will have to do what we can to make it less hard," she said finally. "We have four days. And there is one thing that I can do right now."

With an arm over his shoulders, she led him up the stairs to the attic. Without the odd-colored light, the room was filled with even deeper shadows. Near the window, Abigail bent over the cauldron and jostled some of the sticks beneath it. She blew at them and white, sparkling flames danced up and around the cauldron's sides. With each flicker, the shadows disappeared from one corner of the attic, then another. As they illuminated one wall, John noticed shelves of jars, each containing different leaves and powders. Beside the window, he noticed bouquets of flowers and leaves drying. Tiny black pebbles glinted around the cauldron. The ceiling shivered as the wind hummed outside.

Abigail collected an armful of jars from the shelves. "I have ginger and rose hips and chamomile and," she snapped leaves off a branch, "and a few other things. If you could find a jar of honey, we will have just what we need to make you a proper tonic."

John scanned the labels on the different bottles. "Are they magic?" He sneezed.

Abigail smiled. "No, nothing here is magic. But look there." She pointed to a piece of paper pinned near the window. "That is your formula. The writing is from old Umbra, but I believe I have figured out the general idea. Can you read my notes?"

> Three stones of black from the fire (jet?)
> Three stones of white from the Earth (moonstones?)
> Three stones of green from the ocean (smithsonite -modified)
> Three stones of red from the sky (?)
> Three stones of gold from the stars (umbritite?)

84

"But there are all those questions." John wiped his nose. "Don't you know what it means?"

"I am pretty certain about most of the stones I will need." Abigail struck a match to light a fire beneath the cauldron. "The trouble will be finding the right ones. They will not be anything I could purchase at a store. Evie will have hidden the right stones somewhere."

"You've got three black stones next to your cauldron." John sniffed and pointed down at the fire.

"Those pebbles cannot be important. They have always been here. The stones roll out whenever I set a fire." Abigail stopped, realizing what she had said.

John began to get excited. "Maybe that witch left them for you. Maybe she left them here where they'd be obvious, just so you could get a head start."

Abigail lifted the rocks up into the light. "You know, John Tomas, I believe you are right. These are jet stones. Someone must have carved them specially to make them flat like this. They all have the same five points."

"And you said they come out when you start a fire. They're the stones of black from the fire."

"They must be! I may never have noticed them. But you! You found the first ingredients! You wonderful, wonderful boy!" Abigail swung him around in a hug, juggled the stones in the air, and laughed so hard she nearly cackled – until she dropped one of the stones in the cauldron.

John grinned. "Maybe you should put those somewhere safe."

"Yes." Abigail fished the stone out of the steaming water. "They can stay on the shelf up here while I finish the tonic. We cannot be distracted by this good news. We need to get you healthy and bring Penny home."

85

The air thickened with spices as Abigail stirred added more ingredients to the cauldron. John wiped his nose and looked at the paper again. "You're supposed to puzzle the stones – with all the colors separate. Then boil with powdered kelp/sea lettuce mixture." He turned around. "So you've got to make a potion?"

"I would call it a concoction." Abigail sprinkled flowers into the tonic. "Put those ingredients together with all the magic I can muster, and we will have a terrible explosion. The force of that explosion will carry everything that is not earthly back to Seleumbra."

"Like you and One-Eyed Zach."

"And anyone else from Seleumbra who would like to come along." Abigail glanced out the window again. "I hope Squint found her."

John wasn't worried. He was thinking about the concoction. "Is this potion going to shoot you into the sky? Like a rocket?"

"You could think of it like that." Abigail sounded distracted as she added a lemon to the tonic. "I am hoping to figure everything out in time before the next solar eclipse. At that time, we will see Seleumbra across the entire moon – and in fact, it will be pulling us home just as the concoction is throwing us there. With the power of the eclipse and the explosion, we should find ourselves up and away in no time. It might even be easy."

John laughed and then coughed. "It's a Rocket Concoction."

"That it is." Abigail lifted the bowl from the cauldron and set it on the windowsill. "Or it will be a rocket concoction if we can find everything by the start of summer."

"Is that when we'll have the eclipse?"

"Yes – and by then, we also must find that perfect family for you."

John's head swam. It was a lot to do. They had to teach Abigail to be normal and gather the stones for the concoction. They had to find the perfect family and make Mrs. Collins happy.

"We can do it." Abigail poured purple tonic into a jar and handed it to him. "You have already given me more than Squint and I had since we arrived here. So drink this tonic up while I fill that spotless bathtub for you. Let us see if we can end this afternoon better than we began."

Two New Friends

Penny stumbled down the ocean path with bleary eyes. The wind had grown stronger, but Penny couldn't hear it. The waves were rising high over the rocks, but Penny didn't care. Everything was wrong. Her foot caught on a tree root. She tripped, stopped herself before she could fall, and ran on. Her foot caught on a rock. She tripped again, scraped both of her palms on the gravel, but she picked herself up and kept going. Her foot caught on a log across the path, but this time, she couldn't stop herself. She lurched forward and tumbled off the path. She bumped against every rock and slid through every rose bush before she landed on coarse, wet sand. A wave came and splashed over her legs.

Penny didn't try to keep from crying anymore. Her jacket was dirty, her jeans were ripped, and her knees were torn and bleeding. Penny cried for her cuts and she cried for her clothes. She cried for John and her mother. How much was she supposed to do? she thought.

Over her head, a sea gull cried with her. It landed on the beach and eyed her with beady yellow eyes.

"You there," someone yelled. "Are you hurt?"

Penny wiped her face with fingers covered in sand. A man was running to her in rubber boots that reached over his knees. Penny scowled and wiped her nose. "I'm fine," she said.

Another sea gull sailed over her head and landed on a rock over her shoulder. It called to the first gull, which croaked back an answer.

"You're ok?"

"Yes." Penny felt stupid.

The man dropped a bucket. "You're one of the new kids living on Postman's Hack," he said. "A little late to be walking on a school night, isn't it?"

Penny shrugged.

The man pulled on his nose. "Chilly for May." He crouched in the sand and tipped his bucket so she could see. Inside, with murky water, seaweed and sand, lay a pile of dirty white shells. They clinked when he set the bucket straight. "Thought it seemed about right for some chowder."

Penny pushed herself out of reach from the waves. She wished the man would go away.

"Looks as if you're sitting on a clam yourself there," he said.

Penny checked. She didn't see anything but wet sand and pebbles.

"It's the bubbles." He pointed to a spot near her shoelaces. The sand looked as if it were spitting. "There you'll find one. Go on."

Penny leaned forward. With her hands, she dug a hole in the wet sand. She dug deeper and deeper and almost gave up. Then she saw the ridges of a clamshell. She tugged and the clam fell into her palm. As she brushed the sand off, the shell showed up chalky white.

Penny looked back at the man, who didn't seem surprised.

"Not hard, is it?" He put the clam in his bucket. "We're lucky. Most of Beckon Bay is closed to clamming. Pollution turns the shellfish to poison. Out here, though, there's something special in the water. Charmed, like. Clams can't wait to be found."

He stared out at the ocean. He was older than she first thought. His skin hung loose around his jaw and his eyebrows had grown shaggy and gray. His eyes, though, were strong and icy blue. Penny looked back at the sand. She saw another bubble.

"Mrrow," Squint said, leaping onto one of the rocks. The two sea gulls flapped their wings to fly out of his way.

Penny kept digging for the second clam. "I'm not going back," she told Squint.

"Hrrow," Squint repeated. He came down to investigate the hole. He sniffed and looked up at the man. "Mrrow."

"The cat's trying to tell you something," the man said.

"It's not a cat. It's a buccaneer." Penny made a face. "One-Eyed Zach. But she calls him Squint."

"Fitting."

"It's dumb."

Squint flicked his tail at her.

The man tugged on his nose again. "You got a name?"

She pulled her knees back under her chin. "Penny."

"Joe Cavendish." He pointed down the beach to a little cottage overshadowed by lobster traps. "My place is back there. In front of that new mansion they're building."

"We've seen you on your boat." Penny handed him another clam. "With the sea gulls."

He nodded. "Never far behind, those three. There's Caddy now." A third sea gull flew up from behind the dune grass. "Bill and Burt are the others."

"They all look the same."

"Bill's got the white spot on the tip of his wings. Burt's wings are the darkest." Mr. Cavendish thought for a moment. "Got a brother, haven't you?"

Penny tried to keep her eyes from welling up. "Yeah."

"Long time to be leaving him on his own," Mr. Cavendish observed. "Mostly, I see you two together."

Penny dropped the clam in his bucket. "We aren't going to be together anymore. That woman – the miserable, old Hairy Boar from Social Services, she came today. She said we're a disaster. We've got four more days before she'll take us away."

Mr. Cavendish frowned. ""What she should do, isn't it, if things aren't right."

Penny kicked at the sand. "Abigail is the only one who would take us both together. If we can't stay here, I have to go to a group home for girls. Plus," she glanced Squint, "we promised Abigail. We have to stay and help her. That was the deal."

"The deal, is it?"

"Mrrow," Squint said with his head in the bucket.

"Abigail swore she'd find people to adopt us. She'd get us the perfect family if we'd help her."

Mr. Cavendish grunted. "What kind of help are we talking   about?"

"Teaching her mostly – cooking and cleaning. That kind of stuff."

"Doesn't sound too bad."

91

Penny rolled her eyes. "She doesn't know anything."

Mr. Cavendish pulled on his nose again. "Seems to me that you aren't living up to your side of the bargain. No," he shook his head, "complaining out here isn't going to teach that Abigail a thing. You said you would help. Sounds to me as if you've got to."

Penny thought for a moment and took a deep breath. That was the bargain.

"Besides, I might be able to give you a hand or two." He put his hands on his knees and boosted himself up. "How about I walk you home? I could even teach you how to make real chowder."

Penny took his hand and he helped her up. "Thanks," she said. She meant it.

Two Steps Forward

That evening, Penny and John took seats at the kitchen table with the steamed, sleepy look that comes from hard work, hot baths and fuzzy pajamas. While Mr. Cavendish had inspected the hole in the porch, John had shown Abigail how to peel apples and Penny had mopped the floor. While Penny had rolled out a piecrust, Mr. Cavendish had taught John how to cut the clams out of their shells. From the windowsill, Squint had kept his eye on the chowder as it simmered, yellow butter shining over hot potatoes and cream. From the attic, Abigail had brought everyone jars of purple tonic that smelled warm and sweet and spicy all at once. When finally, they'd scraped the last of the chowder out of their bowls, nobody could keep from feeling full and content.

"You wouldn't think it if you didn't look, but there's potential in this house here," Mr. Cavendish said as he slid a piece of cardboard under a table leg. "I knew the house in the old days. Pretty, it was back then. Bet you could turn it into a real home if you tried."

"It was thanks to Mr. Cavendish that we found the house all those months ago." Abigail cut him another piece of pie. "He knew it had been abandoned."

"Good to have neighbors here again."

"Mr. Cavendish." John had an idea. "Did you know the lady who lived here before? Abigail thinks she hid things – rocks – that are important."

Mr. Cavendish chewed as he tried to remember. "Don't know about her hiding things. I used to see her walking a lot. Loved the fresh air, she used to say."

"Maybe she didn't like being inside this house," Penny said. "It's awfully dark all the time. Plus, things keep exploding."

"The house has its own special spirit, I find." Abigail sipped her tonic. "With the humming and creaking, the house seems to be talking. That oven certainly tells me something each time I go near it."

Penny shot a look at Abigail. "You aren't saying that on top of everything else, the house is haunted?"

"Is it?" John nearly choked on a bite of pie. "Do we have ghosts?"

Squint leaped onto the table. "Mrrow," he said, but Abigail tossed him back onto the floor before he could lick her piece of pie.

"Scratch me again and you will not get anything," Abigail told him. "And John Tomas, I doubt we have ghosts. At least, I have yet to meet one."

"House can't be haunted now with you here to liven things up." Mr. Cavendish scanned the kitchen. "Even starting to look friendly here."

"It's not bad with the floors clean," Penny admitted.

"Put some of your pictures on the wall and it'll look better," Mr. Cavendish said. "Like you two are settling in. Might impress someone coming to see how you're coping."

"Penny can do that," John said. "She can make really good pictures."

Abigail's face glowed. "Penelope Rose, please do."

Penny felt uncomfortable. "My pictures aren't that good."

"Get the idea across, won't they?" Mr. Cavendish said. "'Specially if you drew something cheerful. Happy kids make happy pictures. Inspectors couldn't argue with that."

Shadows swooped in front of the window onto the grass. Penny tilted her head to watch the seagulls strut back and forth. Their wings seemed to have taken colors from the sunset. "It's Caddy, isn't it? And Burt." Penny pointed the seagulls out to John, "Bill's the other one. You can tell them apart when they fly."

"They're telling me I've got an early morning tomorrow." Mr. Cavendish climbed to his feet. "We've got to be on our way."

Abigail stood up to hold his coat for him. "We are very grateful to you for keeping Penelope Rose company. And for making us dinner. It was delicious."

John stood up, too. "Thanks for the clams," he said, holding out his hand.

Mr. Cavendish shook it gravely. "Bring you lobster next time." He looked over at Squint, finishing

94

Abigail's pie. "And if the buccaneer would like to join us on the water tomorrow, he's welcome."

Awkwardly, Penny got to her feet. "Thanks for — you know."

Mr. Cavendish put on his hat. "Tell me how it goes this week." He nodded to her and then, taking his bucket, he left with his boots squelching on the floor.

The screen door slammed. Caddy and Burt flew up over the pine trees.

"We're going to have to clean the floor again." Penny counted the mud prints Mr. Cavendish had left behind. "And there's that hole in the porch we'll have to fix."

"Leave that to me," Abigail said. "First, I will demonstrate how well I learned to tidy a kitchen. You need to prepare for school tomorrow."

"You've got to stay out of trouble," John told Penny.

"And you've got to start talking." Penny sighed. "But tonight, you'd better quiz me on my spelling words. And I'll check your homework. That old Hairy Boar will see that we won't flunk out of school."

Two Reasons To Tidy Up

At school the next day, John raised his hand twice, even though Mrs. Sok only called on him once. He raced through worksheets of adding problems and even solved a math puzzle Mrs. Sok gave him.

"Not everyone can see how to fold this paper into a three dimensional shape," Mrs. Sok said, leaning on his shoulder as she picked up the puzzle. "Class, remember how we talked about pentagons last week? John glued twelve pentagons together to make a ball.

Watt, please keep your comments to yourself. It may look like a soccer ball, but it is called a dodecahedron. John did a very nice job."

John impressed his teacher, but down the hall, Mr. Keenes didn't pay any attention to Penny. She liked it better that way. If he didn't notice her, he couldn't tell Mrs. Collins anything bad.

"Bring up your homework," Mr. Keenes said. "No talking."

"Hello, Henny-Penny," Caitlin said sweetly as Penny walked to her seat. A funny smell hung in the air. "Nice outfit."

Penny slid into the chair, but she was sure she smelled something suspicious. She checked her chair to make sure nobody had stuck gum on it. She checked the bottom of her desk to be certain there wasn't a trap. Then she heard little clicks inside her desk. Carefully, she lifted the lid.

She had to put her hand in front of her mouth to keep from crying out. A green crab scuttled across her science book. Behind him, he dragged a wet piece of seaweed. Penny closed her desk and smiled as nicely as she could at Caitlin. It would take more than a rock-colored crab to get her in trouble that day.

But the kids in her class didn't stop trying. Caitlin said Penny was cheating when they had a quiz in spelling, but that didn't work because Penny could spell the words out loud without looking. When Tony said she was typing swears on the computer, Penny could show that she was searching for electricians on the Internet. Caitlin spilled milk all over Penny's pastrami and peach sandwich and Tony used her apple as a baseball. Still, Penny never did anything back, no matter how much she wanted to. Another day, she'd get even with Caitlin and Tony big time. But for the next three days, Penny had to stay out of trouble.

When Abigail met them after school, she told Penny and John that she'd made progress on her own. "Squint went off with Mr. Cavendish, so I managed to clean the little bathroom downstairs and sweep all the floors. If you help me with the rest, Mrs. Collins will not be able to recognize the house."

The clear sky made the clouds snowy white, the ocean azure blue, and the rocks slate gray. Abigail paused to watch two sailboats tack around a fort in the harbor. John squatted down to see a barnacle reach out its tentacles for food in a tide pool. Penny opened her backpack and lifted out a heart-shaped pencil box she'd taken from Caitlin's desk. Inside, looking sick, was the crab. She dropped it over John's shoulder into the tide pool and it scuttled out of sight.

"What would you think if we made a bouquet?" Abigail regarded the beach roses peeping pink around their leaves. "We could have flowers and grasses from the garden outside."

"We could put sea shells on the mantle." Penny held up a slipper shell just tinged with pink.

"And your pictures on the wall," John said.

"It will be beautiful," Abigail predicted.

The house did not make it easy, however. As Abigail swept cobwebs from the ceiling, the walls shuddered plaster onto the mantle Penny had just wiped. When John tried to dust the old paintings, the floor sagged and toppled him off his stool.

"You'd think the house didn't want to be fixed up," Penny said while she struggled to peel the rug off the floor. "Those paintings look just as dirty as they were before John dusted them."

John stood back. "The paintings aren't yours, are they, Abigail?"

"They were here when we arrived." Abigail stepped over Penny to see. "They must be very old. The harbor does not look like that anymore. And that other painting must have been made of our house just after it was built."

"The picture on that wall is the beach by Mr. Cavendish's house." Penny sat back on her heels. "The rocks lean forward towards the ocean like that."

"On the frames, it says something." John pointed out. "See – right under the picture of the house. 'Do not hold onto what you find first.' And the one of the beach says, 'Find three in the sea where you lose your direction.'"

"How funny," Abigail said. "The words under the harbor painting are very similar: 'Three there in the air where you swirl all direction.'"

Penny stood up to examine a watercolor of a farm. "'Fields of rubies hide buried treasure,'" John read over her shoulder, "'where the lighthouse disappears.'"

Abigail pointed to a sketch in pen and ink. "That frame there does not say anything at all. Perhaps it is too small, just that lonely island with a single tree."

"Maybe that's why they had to sew a motto over here. 'Time gives golden treasures when it is time.'"

Penny turned away from the needlepoint on the opposite wall. "None of them make any sense."

"What if they aren't supposed to make sense?" John reread them all with his brows furrowed. "What if they belonged to Evie? She might have left them behind as clues. They could be for the rocket concoction."

"It is possible, John Tomas." Abigail thought for a moment. "Only how could we find a place to swirl all direction?"

"Or lose your direction?"

"We won't find a field of rubies near here." Penny went back to rolling up the rug. "There couldn't be a bunch of jewels lying around that nobody's dug up already."

The little clock whirred and pinged four bells. This time, when the doors opened, the little men danced with white semi-circles.

"Mrrow." Squint sprang onto the mantle.

"Stop right there," Abigail told him. "In fact, you can turn around and take those fish bones outside. We are trying to clean up."

But Squint wasn't very interested in preparing for Mrs. Collins' inspection or even hearing about the clues. As John carried sofa cushions to the back porch, Squint pawed at the tassels to see the dust shake down on the floor. When Penny swept cobwebs onto the porch, Squint batted the spiders through the dirt piles.

"Vile animal." Abigail stomped a foot at him. "Look at what you have done to my clean floors. You had better be eating those spiders when you catch them."

Penny shut the front door gently to avoid another shower of plaster. "Do you think he can catch beetles? There are hundreds in the closets upstairs."

"Did you hear her, cat? The beetles, too, in the closets upstairs." Abigail went after Squint, but she stopped at the kitchen doorway. "You pirate! Look at what those dirty paws did!"

John pulled open the screen door just in time to allow Squint escape into the backyard. "Oh," John said. Smudged paw prints speckled the floor.

"This is ridiculous," Abigail said. Muttering to herself, she began to fill a bucket with more water and soap.

John went back outside to the sofa cushions on the porch. Against his legs, he felt the air move, softer than a wind but stronger than a breeze. Suddenly, Squint howled. John leaped back. With a bitter look in his eye, Squint floated up out of the grass in the garden. The air carried him up the back steps, past John and through the door that Abigail held open.

"It is time, Zecharias Murdock Boreas Finn, for you to start contributing," Abigail said. "Penelope Rose would like you to help with the beetles upstairs."

Squint hissed at her, but the air jerked him by the scruff of his neck and carried him out of the kitchen. Meanwhile, the mop flew out of the pantry and dipped itself in the bucket. It spun to wring itself and slowly began to wipe the spots off the floor.

John swallowed. "You aren't supposed to be using magic."

Abigail sighed. "I know. But we have too much to do, even if Squint does behave himself. There is dinner to make and homework to do. And you and Penelope Rose need to be rested for school tomorrow."

They heard Penny cry out as Squint floated past her. Running down the hallway, she demanded, "What are you doing? You said you had to conserve your strength."

"I will be fine." Abigail waved an arm at the mop, which flew about in a circle before landing with a soggy plop. "This is a small attempt to move us along. I shall continue to work with you the normal way. I need one of you to teach me how to clean the furniture."

The mop dipped itself back in the bucket. John's sofa cushions flew over his head and then over Penny's on their return to the living room. John grabbed the last one before it sailed away. "I'm not done with this one yet," he said, heading for the backyard.

"It's your call," Penny told Abigail. "If you want to use magic, it's your choice. Only we're sticking to our part of the bargain. You've still got to find us that perfect family, even if you use up all your powers."

"I remember. I still want to get home."

With a nod, Penny returned to work. As rags wiped dust off the furniture, she sponged the front stairs clean. While John showed Abigail how to polish the old dining room table, the rug upstairs shook itself out a window. The mop finished the kitchen, the broom finished the front room and Penny finished the back stairs. John cleaned the windows, Penny dusted the shelves and Abigail brought them chowder for dinner. Hour after hour they worked, growing hot and sticky and covered in grime. Abigail's face turned pea green, but when the clock chimed eight times, she pulled herself to her feet and regarded the stairwell with triumph.

"That is enough," she called to Penny in the small bedroom and John in the big bedroom. "You are going to stop, take hot baths and tackle your homework. Mrs. Collins will not believe what we have managed to accomplish."

Penny wiped her eyes. John wiped his forehead. Their shoulders ached, their backs were sore and their hands were rough, red and wrinkled. But in the nighttime shadows of the pine trees, large boulders rose up from the ocean and settled themselves in place of the rotten boards of the front porch. The windows reflected the white light of the crescent moon. And in the living room, the inscriptions on the old picture frames glimmered like polished gold.

Two Reasons To Celebrate

At the end of the week, every kid and teacher wanted to run right into weekend. New leaves stretched lush and green in warm sunshine. Soft wind carried the perfume of spring flowers. Summer was coming, but Penny and John did not think about vacations or flowers or baseball or camp. Penny and John spent the entire day worrying about Mrs. Collins' inspection.

They met Abigail and Squint on the back steps of the house. "We have been outside all afternoon," Abigail said, trying not to sound nervous. "After you left this morning, I thought to show Mrs. Collins how I learned to make French toast. Then I dropped the carton of eggs and spilled most of the milk. Squint, of course, was most unhelpful. It took me three tries to get the floor clean again. But I believe Mrs. Collins will be impressed. See, I dressed up."

She held out her arms and spun around. Penny sighed. It looked as if Abigail had slept in her clothes.

"Just like Mrs. Collins," Abigail said. "Of course, Squint is not pleased."

John looked around. Hiding under the porch steps, Squint clawed at a red ribbon around his neck.

"He looks mad," John said.

"He can stay mad," Abigail said. "It is about time he did something helpful. Today, I expect him to act like a real pet."

102

Squint hissed, but they all started when the doorbell rang. "There she is," Abigail said, adding a final wrinkle to her skirt. "No need to worry, John Tomas. I am sure everything will be fine."

But everything was not fine inside the house.

"You didn't forget to turn off the oven again, did you?" Penny grabbed potholders and coughed through the smoke.

"There's something stuck to the floor in the hallway," John said.

Squint howled as he tripped over his ribbon.

"Miss McKinney," Mrs. Collins called from behind the door, "I am not going to wait forever!"

"Bother." Muttering under her breath, Abigail walked to the front of the house. Behind her, a gust of wind pushed open the back door. As Penny lifted a smoking tray out of the oven, the wind swept it from her hands and tossed it into the garden. Another gust yanked up the egg stuck to the hallway floor and pulled the ribbon from around Squint's neck. Once the screen door slammed shut, Abigail took a deep breath and pulled open the front door.

"Welcome," she said.

"You're looking odd again." Mrs. Collins hiked up her dress to scratch at a scab on her knee. "Green, I'd say. Not going to throw up, are you?" She grunted at Penny and John as she limped forward. "Still wearing the same clothes you wore at the shelter, I see. They wondered at school if anyone here does laundry."

A breeze rose up through the open windows and jerked the doorknob out Abigail's hand. As the door slammed, a dusting of powdered plaster showered onto Penny and John's shoulders.

"As I thought." Mrs. Collins brushed past them. "It is impossible to stay clean in this place."

Mrs. Collins hobbled through the house, her nostrils wide to sniff out anything odd. Clearly, she said, Abigail had spoiled the children with the fancy bedroom – the gurgling toilet was desperate for repair – and what was that burned smell in the kitchen? Yet when they returned to the new stone steps, Mrs. Collins almost nodded.

"I'll grant you, this is much better than I expected," she said. "The picture of pirates shooting at that pig – that is rather odd, but Missy here does seem to have made an effort. I hear Buster even thanked his teacher on the way out of school yesterday. No, I had been warned to expect much worse."

Penny had to be careful not to roll her eyes. John was afraid to look up. Squint tried to purr, but it sounded more as if he had gas.

"And the house didn't collapse," Mrs. Collins said.

"Yes." Abigail bit her lip. "Yes, I am very sorry about the other day."

Mrs. Collins snorted. "I haven't enjoyed coming out here again and again. There are twenty new files on my desk. Half of those kids would be happy to take your places, even here." She eyed Penny and John. "You have made improvements, I'll admit, so I'll keep my word. If you're willing to put up with one another, then I'll leave things as they are for now. But you two had better be models for other delinquents. If I hear one more thing about you causing trouble or doing anything odd, I'll move you immediately. No more chances. "

"Yes," Abigail said. "Yes, of course." It didn't sound as if she knew what she was saying.

104

"Humph." Without saying good-bye, Mrs. Collins limped down to her car. Without looking back, she drove away. Abigail stood frozen with Penny and John on the boulders that held up the new front porch.

"We can stay?" John asked. He looked back at Penny. "She isn't coming back?"

"Sounds like it." Penny kept her voice steady, but inside, something joyous bubbled.

"It does." Abigail repeated, still in shock. "I suppose – it is true, then – that we passed the test. We will stay together."

"Hurrah!" John said. He swung onto the porch railing and slid down. Squint followed, leaping onto John's shoulders. "Hurrah!" John shouted. "Hurrah!"

Penny swallowed a laugh that wanted to come out for no reason at all. Abigail looked as if she were trying not to cry.

They all turned around at a voice calling from the kitchen.

"Hey, there," Mr. Cavendish called. "Anyone home?"

"Mr. Cavendish!" John raced down the hallway. "We can stay! We're going to be models for delinquents!"

Mr. Cavendish put a large plastic tray on the kitchen counter. "I knew you'd do fine."

"Did you catch those?" John bounded up to look at the five blue and green-spotted lobsters crawling around in water in the tray.

"Thought I might invite myself to dinner. There's one extra for the buccaneer if he'd like it."

"How kind of you," Abigail said, following Penny into the kitchen. "Squint may be the only one among us who has ever eaten lobster before."

Squint leaped onto John's shoulders to choose his lobster, while Mr. Cavendish directed Penny to find the largest pot in the kitchen. "And what about the hole in the steps?" he asked.

Penny and John interrupted one another to tell him about Mrs. Collins' inspection. Meanwhile, he filled the pot with water and salt and put it on the stove. "Pretty impressive work for a couple of days," Mr. Cavendish said. "I should get you to clean up my place."

"We're not done here," Penny said. "We still need to get an electrician – and a plumber."

"The toilet burps," John explained.

Mr. Cavendish leaned against the counter. "That's not a problem. Even I could help you there."

"We'd pay you," Penny offered. "Somehow, I mean."

Abigail looked up from setting the table. "I can get another job."

"No matter what, you're going to need to get another job. Mal won't let us work for groceries again." Penny turned to Mr. Cavendish. "We couldn't do anything for you, could we? We could work on weekends if you'd help with the plumbing and stuff."

"I was serious about you cleaning up my place before. And I could always use a hand on my boat now and then."

"We can do that," John said.

"Let's see." Mr. Cavendish lifted him up so John could reach inside the tray. "Grab hold of a lobster – by his back there. I'll do the knife part. And now drop him in the pot, claws first. Don't worry, all this kills them quick." He nodded as John reached for another lobster. "There you go. We'll make a lobsterman out of you."

Penny wrinkled her nose, but Abigail was fascinated. "They're turning red, just like magic."

"Come to think of it, I saw that the Magic Shop is looking for help." Mr. Cavendish put John on the floor. "Could motor you into town tomorrow morning. Start a working account for you kids, too, if you agree to help me with my traps along the way."

"Sure," Penny said.

"It'll be fun."

"And I am certain I could work at a Magic Shop." Abigail spun John around. "Everything is going splendidly."

John threw himself into her arms. "We're going to stay together!"

"Just like a family!" Abigail gave him a hug.

"A screwy family," Penny said. She and Mr. Cavendish watched Abigail and John jig around the kitchen. Out the window, they could see Squint bound off to play with Bill and Burt. The seagulls shrieked, Abigail cackled and John laughed out loud. Penny winced. "They're all crazy," she said.

"Wouldn't say that." Mr. Cavendish pulled on his nose. He grinned as Abigail swung John high in the air. "Never had much family to count on myself. Lost the only girl I'd wanted. Never thought I'd find another to take her place. Come to be my age and you'll find that friends aren't easy to come by neither, not when there's trouble or hard work.

"No," he nodded at Abigail and John, "you're lucky to have folks who need you to look after them – and folks who'll look after you. Even old sea dogs know they don't want to be out on their own when a storm comes up."

He reached down the counter to hand Penny a stick of butter. "Melt that and you'll understand what Bill is screaming about out there."

Later, after they'd settled down on the back steps, after they'd dipped the lobster meat in melted butter and sucked the bits out of the little lobster legs, Penny and John agreed. It did feel like the start of a good weekend.

Two Members of a Crew

The next morning, Penny and John had to wake up even earlier than they did for school. Just as the sun began to change the color of the sky, Abigail poured them cereal. Before they had rubbed the sleep from their eyes, she helped them into sweaters and jackets. In the meantime, Squint moved from the tabletop to the windowsill in order to make a full weather report.

"Mrrow," he said.

"Yes, yes, we are coming," Abigail said as she rushed Penny and John upstairs to brush their teeth. "We cannot be late for our first day on the water."

They found Mr. Cavendish waiting on the beach with an old wooden dinghy. Caddy flew over his head, testing the wind. "Morning," Mr. Cavendish said, handing them orange life vests. Awkwardly, they swung legs over the sides of the rowboat and forward over lines of wet rope. The smell of old fish and salt air made Penny blink her eyes and the wind made John sit up and breathe deeply. Squint perched at the front of the dinghy and called to Mr. Cavendish to shove off. Mr. Cavendish, in rubber pants that reached above his waist, pushed the dinghy deeper into the water before he swung aboard. With a rumble, he started the motor and in seconds, everyone's face was sprinkled with salt.

Squint began singing in a joyful, horrible yowl until Abigail yanked his tail.

"Any more of that and I will push you overboard," she said, looking queasy as the dinghy bumped along. "Cats do not swim here, do they, John Tomas?"

Squint flicked his tail at her.

"That there's Caddy's," Mr. Cavendish said, nodding to a small red lobster boat with *Caddy* painted in white letters across the hull.

"Why didn't you name it after the other seagulls?" Penny asked. She had to shout over the buzz of the motor.

"Seems more like Caddy's boat than mine." Mr. Cavendish pointed. While Bill and Burt played up and down in the wind, Caddy had already begun to inspect the gear. "I picked up lobstering only after I retired. Found Caddy over near your place. That bird's taught me more than anyone in the harbor."

Mr. Cavendish motored the dinghy to the stern of the boat, where the hull was lower. Squint jumped right onboard, but everyone else had to scramble from one rocking boat to another. As Mr. Cavendish climbed up, he kept hold of the dinghy so he could tie it to the mooring. "That'll be your job next time," he told John. "Dinghy drifts off from that pink balloon there and we'll be swimming home."

John nodded vigorously. "I can do it."

"Show me. Crawl up to the bow and get us unattached."

Squint gave John instructions, while Mr. Cavendish turned to Penny. "Let's see if you can get us going. Turn the key there and start the motor. Then pull down on the lever. That's it. Off we go."

The *Caddy* shuddered and coughed before puttering out of the cove into Beckon Bay. Before she could stop herself, Penny grinned at Abigail, who held onto her stomach and tried to smile back. "Well done, Penelope Rose," Abigail said faintly. "I will just sit down next to you and keep out of the way. Is the boat really supposed to toss around like this?"

Penny laughed. She couldn't help it. With the sun on the horizon, the ocean looked like melted silver. The trees on the islands were just starting to emerge out of shadows. John stayed up at the bow of the boat with his legs swinging over the hull. Mr. Cavendish gave Penny directions towards Safe Haven.

"Slow down here," Mr. Cavendish told her. "And stop. The red buoy here's my first."

John pointed up towards shore. "There's our house."

"And here's your next job." Mr. Cavendish waved him back to the stern. "There are three traps down there. They'll be heavy, so I'll do the pulling. You're in charge of the gaff."

He handed John a long hook and helped John yank up the line that attached the buoy to the traps in the water. Mr. Cavendish took the buoy and pulled the line up and over the hauler. Next, he turned on a small motor, which cranked the line higher out of the water.

Caddy cried out and swooped over the line. "I can see the first trap!" John shouted.

The water was murky green, but out of the shadows came a large metal lobster trap. Mr. Cavendish stopped the motor and, even though he was white-haired and wrinkled, he pulled the trap onto the washboard easily.

"There's a lobster!" Penny rushed over before she could help herself.

"How wonderful." Abigail bent over her knees with her eyes closed. "Just tell me when it is time to go home."

Mr. Cavendish put on heavy rubber gloves. "The lobster will get you if you let it. That's why you wear your gloves and pick it up by its back."

"And that's why you put rubber bands over the claws." John hopped up and down. "I could do that."

Mr. Cavendish handed John a clamp to stretch the thick rubber bands over the lobster's claws. Afterwards, he handed him a metal gauge with a notch at one end. "Stick that in the eye socket. If the bug's not big enough, his back won't reach down to that mark there. Nope, we're fine."

Mr. Cavendish handed the lobster to Penny to put in a tank. Bill and Burt squawked until he tossed them the bits of crab left in the trap. More patient, Caddy caught a small fish that Mr. Cavendish threw to her on the cabin roof. "There's breakfast," he said.

Penny thought she needed to be ready at the wheel to move on, but Mr. Cavendish called her over to the hauler. "You get to do the next one," he said and sure enough, the pulley cranked up another trap.

They went through the process again and again, through three traps on the first trawl, five on the next, and more after that. Abigail tried to imagine herself back on land, but Squint, Penny and John had a great time out on the water. By the time Mr. Cavendish took over the motor to steer into harbor, Penny and John could handle any job he'd given to them.

"Why don't you three walk around and see what jobs you can find," Mr. Cavendish said as he heaved the first tray of lobsters onto the dock. "The buccaneer here can help me clean up. By the time you're through, we should be ready for lunch."

Abigail stumbled off the boat and up to the pier. Squint and Mr. Cavendish headed to a warehouse to negotiate a price for the catch. But Penny and John lingered on the dock. They could see the brick buildings of Safe Haven standing proud and familiar on the street. Below the pier, however, hid a world they didn't recognize. Pilings clumped and gathered like a dank, leafless forest. The air smelled of old fish, stale water, and diesel fuel. Only splotches of sunlight reached the greasy water. It wasn't pretty, and nobody came down from the town unless they had to.

But at the end of the dock, in the shadows of the pier, hid a shop.

"That's funny," Penny said.

"We've never seen that before," John said.

Two Losses

Once a sign must have stood over the shop window. Once the window must have been washed. But now, all they could see through a dim veil of dust and grime, were rows and shelves of bottles: old soda bottles, old medicine bottles, bottles wider than John and bottles taller than Penny.

John moved closer. "That one is like the bottle I found," he said. "That green one." Out of his pocket, John took the little blue bottle he'd found on the rocks. Both bottles had the same swirls of letters across the body.

"Yours is smaller," Penny said, peering into the window. Where a flash of light touched a bottle, the glass shone in brilliant colors: emerald, gold and garnet. Penny saw perfume bottles with tasseled stoppers and perfume bottles so impossibly thin, they seemed to be made out of flower petals. One little golden jar seemed to wink at her with a violet swirl. Penny looked closer, and made a face. Beside the golden jar stood a jar of dead rats in preservatives.

"Like bottles, do you?" A gaunt, pasty-faced man slouched in the doorway. A toothpick dangled from his mouth, and he hadn't washed or cut his hair for a long time. "Choose any bottle you like and I will give you a fair trade. That is why they call me The Trader."

"We don't need any bottles," Penny said.

"But you would like one, I bet." The Trader's eyes gleamed as he regarded the bottle in John's hand. "What about you, boy-o? How would you like me to trade you a model ship? I have one, full-rigged and ready to sail." The Trader used his toothpick to point out a schooner resting on a pile of tiny blue pebbles in a bottle.

John couldn't imagine how anyone could have built the boat in the bottle. He couldn't see how someone could fit the polished wheel at the helm. John would have loved to have the boat in the bottle, but he shook his head. They didn't have any money.

"It would not cost you a nickel." The Trader's voice sounded smooth and silky. "I notice that you have a bottle handy. We could work out a trade. Your pretty blue bottle for my model ship."

Penny looked from one bottle to the other. "Why would you trade that fancy boat for John's little one? It doesn't seem fair."

"True," said The Trader. "I would not consider it unless it had its original cap. Complete, it might be

114

worth something to someone." The Trader paused. "You do have the top, I assume. A screw cap, maybe, or a stopper?"

Slowly, John pulled the twist of wires from his pocket. He hadn't noticed before, but the stopper was heavier than it should have been for an empty twist of wires.

The Trader slid around the door to the window. "We could make a sort of wager," he said, draping an arm over John's shoulder. "If you win, each of you may choose a bottle, any you like. You will not have to give me a thing."

"And if John loses?" Penny was suspicious.

"It is an easy enough game." With his toothpick, The Trader counted out bottles lined up before the schooner. "There are seventeen bottles between that perfume bottle and the one with the boat. You count over one, two or three bottles. Then I count over one, two or three bottles. You count, I count – until one of us has to pick up that last bottle."

Penny made a face. The last bottle was full of fish bones. "John won't want that one."

"Pick that and you lose the wager, boy-o. Force me to choose the bottle of bones and you get two bottles of your choice. It sounds like a good trade to me."

John's eyes moved from his little blue bottle to the schooner in the shop window. He weighed the wire stopper in his hand. He wanted all of them.

"You don't have to play," Penny told him. She didn't trust The Trader.

"You have nothing to be afraid of." The Trader grinned. "Go on. You can choose first."

John glanced at Penny, who shrugged. Then he took a deep breath and pointed at the first bottle. The

Trader counted over two, John counted over three, The Trader counted two, John counted two, The Trader counted two and held up his hands. "You lose," he said. "No matter what you choose, you will have to pick the last bottle."

"No," John said.

"Wait a minute," Penny said.

But it was true. John had lost his bottle.

The Trader twirled the little blue bottle around in his fingers. He dropped the stopper in his pocket "Not a bad trade," he said.

John clenched his fists. He didn't mean to lose the bottle from Seleumbra. He hadn't wanted to lose the stopper. He thought about the game and thought about the counting. He had made a mistake, but he didn't know how.

Penny didn't care. "That's not fair," she said. "You knew he'd lose."

"Nobody forced him to play." The Trader began to slink into his shop, but a voice stopped him.

"Penelope Rose? John Tomas?" Abigail leaned over the pier. "What are you doing down there? I thought you said the shops are in town."

"Well, now," The Trader said, craning his long neck. "Do you belong to these two?"

"You have my new family down there." Abigail shaded her eyes. "Penelope Rose, are you coming?"

"Not yet." Penny put her hands on hips and glared at The Trader. "We're not going anywhere until you let us play again. John shouldn't have lost his bottle. It wasn't fair."

"I never said the game was fair." The Trader glanced up at Abigail. "I suppose, as a favor, we can play again for your bottle. But if you lose this time, you will owe me a favor. Got it?"

John nodded. He nodded and thought. He thought some more and then he beamed at Penny. He saw the trick. He knew how to win. "This time," he said, "Trader, you count first."

The Trader whistled softly. He counted three of the bottles. This time, John thought carefully and counted one. The Trader counted two, John counted one, The Trader counted three and John took a deep breath. Finally, he counted two. Then he smiled triumphantly. "You lose."

"You are smart enough when you think, boy-o." The Trader tossed him the little blue bottle from Seleumbra. "In the future, you should look to the end before you begin."

"You forgot to give him the stopper," Penny pointed out.

"I never said anything about returning the stopper." The Trader stepped back into the shadows. "Just the bottle. Be grateful for that." He shut his door. They heard the lock turn.

"Hm," Penny said.

"I shouldn't have played the game." John kicked a lobster claw into the water. "It was a trick, just like you said."

"At least you figured it out. And you got the bottle back."

"I lost the stopper."

"But Abigail said the stopper didn't come from Seleumbra. So it's not like it's important."

"I guess." John frowned as he pocketed the bottle. "But I want it back."

"Yeah." Penny glanced back over her shoulder. "It's strange that he kept it."

"Come along, slowpokes." Abigail waved them up to the pier. "You can talk later. We need to find the Magic Shop."

Two More Introductions

Abigail loved Safe Haven, she told Penny and John once they joined her up in the sunshine. She loved the cobblestones and the old, narrow side streets. She loved the shiny boutique windows and the old brick warehouses. But most of all, she loved the Magic Shop. It had a Help Wanted sign in the window.

"And it is magic," Abigail whispered to John, "just as Mr. Cavendish said. I can do magic!"

"You said you wanted to do things normally," Penny reminded her. "That means no magic."

Penny pushed open the door and inhaled a whiff of incense. John stumbled through a tangle of tapestries hanging from the ceiling. Once he was free, he saw a woman, wider than a doorway, fling her arms open.

"Welcome, darlings, welcome! You look like you could use some Magic. What about moisturizer? A new

118

dress, maybe? Jewelry?" She spun a rack of bangles around so they could see the sparkle. "Or why not a hat?" She flung a feathered cap on John's head. "What do you think?"

John's voice, muffled by the brim, said something sounding like, "No, thanks."

Penny choked on a giggle. Abigail beamed broadly. The woman laughed hard enough to make her whole body jiggle.

"That's right," the woman said, wiping her eyes. "Let it out, my dears. If I can give you a good laugh, then I haven't wasted your time. My name is Magic and I am here to help."

"Oh!" Abigail said. "That is why you call it the Magic Shop."

"That's right." Magic reached over and squeezed Abigail's hand. "Hon, some folks stop by looking for wands and things, but really what they want is happiness. And that, I try to give them." She lifted a feather to look down at John. "Do you want some happiness, my love?"

"We want a job," Penny said. "The sign said you were hiring."

Magic looked distressed. "I'm sorry, sweetheart. I'd welcome your help, but I have to hire someone older."

"We're not looking for us – for her."

"Of course!" Magic gave Penny a hug that felt like it was made of pillows. "For her, I have plenty of jobs! Has she ever worked in a store before?"

"No," Penny said.

But Abigail interrupted. "Yes, I have. I worked at Mal's Market. And for a short time, I worked at the Clam Counter."

Magic gave Abigail a hug, too, squishing Abigail and Penny together. "Wonderful! I need someone who knows about working in stores and making people happy. Unfortunately, there's a bit of tidying involved. Nobody seems to like that part."

Abigail's eyes lit up. "I can wash dishes."

Magic laughed again. "There won't be many dishes to wash, but there's always a pile of dresses to hang. You'll be busy, but cutie, I hope you'll be happy."

Arm in arm, Magic walked Penny and Abigail through the shop. She pointed out the jewelry from China, sweaters from Guatemala, and dresses from India. She had them compare Italian perfumes, Moroccan leathers and Egyptian oils.

With a tinkle of bells, the shop door opened.

"Hello," a woman said in a low, lilting voice with the curl of an accent. "Hello, there. Would any of you be able to show me –"

"Come in!" Magic waved a handful of scarves at her. "Come in and be welcome! We can show you anything you like. Feather boas! Tangerine lip-gloss! And my new assistant –Aberdeen – "

"Abigail."

"—Abby here could outfit you in whichever sunhat you choose." Magic squeezed Abigail's hand. "You can do it. It will be your first customer."

"Yes." Abigail took a deep breath and tried to fling a straw hat over the woman's head. It landed on John instead. "Bother," Abigail said. "Magic makes it look so easy."

"Not to worry." Amused, the woman winked as she took the hat from his head. "I'm afraid I can't shop today. I was to meet my film crew ten minutes ago."

"But we can't let you leave without a handbag. It's perfect for a safari. No, no, don't be modest." Magic chuckled. "Dearie, we watch you all the time on TV: *Daphne Davis Tames the Wild*. My precious partner loves watching you in the jungle. Monkeys may climb on top of your assistants, but you always look so trim and pretty."

"How kind you are. Oh, but the blouse is silk –" Mrs. Davis lost her balance as Magic gave her a hug. "Yes, you're very kind. Thank you. It is lovely to meet a fan. Now could you possibly tell me where I'd find the library?"

"But you haven't tried these on." Magic reached for a pair of slippers resembling moose heads.

A phone in Mrs. Davis' purse began to chirp. "No, I've got to run."

"But you'd look adorable in this." Magic held out a cap with lobster claws attached to the sides.

"Maybe another time." Mrs. Davis reached for the door.

"Abigail, you can help her." Penny nudged Abigail forward. "She'll be your first customer. Just tell her the library is up a few blocks. Take a left at city hall and it's right there. You know." She poked Abigail again.

"Yes." Abigail shook herself. "Certainly. Just a few minutes away." She glanced back at Penny. "Yes, that should be right."

"Perfect." Mrs. Davis winked at Penny as she answered her cell phone. "Hello? Yes, I'm finally on my way. Thank you, Aberdeen. Good luck with your new job."

"Well done!" Magic exclaimed when the door closed behind her. "One happy customer – and a celebrity, too. You know her husband, don't you, my

121

dears? He's Trey Davis, the man who opened those big toy stores. I hear he's building her a cottage on the water. And now she's coming into my shop!" Magic nearly suffocated Abigail with one last hug. "Honey-pie, I should have known you would bring me luck the minute you walked in!"

Two Points of View

Once Abigail got the job at the Magic Shop, Penny expected life to settle down. At school, at least, she had a routine. Penny had to avoid sea urchins on her chair, gum beneath her desk, and any note or book that appeared mysteriously in her vicinity. Whenever Mr. Keenes asked a hard question, Penny knew he would call on her first. Whenever he lined students up, she knew he would call her last. Penny hated school as much as ever, but during recess at least, she could slip into the library and study ocean charts for Mr. Cavendish. And at lunch, she could sit with John.

"So why wouldn't The Trader give you back the stopper?" Penny wondered out loud for the fourth time that week. "It's like he wanted the stopper more than the bottle."

"Abigail said the stopper wasn't special." John took a bite of his pickle and peach sandwich. Abigail still didn't understand how to make a normal lunch, but sometimes her mistakes didn't taste bad. "What I don't get is the whole 'Three in the sea where you lose your direction.' You could get lost anywhere on the ocean if you didn't have a compass or map or something. We just did compasses in science."

"I wouldn't mind finding a field of rubies." Penny closed the lid on her apple and cabbage salad. "But I don't know how we could do that either. The whole thing is weird to me."

"You know what I think is weird?" Watt poked John in the back. "All that stuff coming out your window last week. Why won't you tell us what happened? We saw the broom and everything."

John shrank back. Watt and Hank asked him questions every day and he never knew what to say. "Nothing happened," John said.

"Don't you guys have your own places to sit?" Penny asked. "Go find your own table and leave us alone."

"But it was amazing!" Hank shoved his way onto the bench next to John. "That flying carpet and everything! We've watched and watched, but we haven't seen it happen again. Doesn't the witch ever take you for a ride?"

"We'd make her take us," Watt said. "We'd bring the witch pickled onions and she'd fly us to Hong Kong."

"You think, Watt? You think we could go to Mexico, too?"

"She's not a witch." But John didn't sound convincing.

"Go away." Penny stood up so they knew she was serious. "We've got enough to worry about without you getting in the way."

John knew Penny was worried about money and Mrs. Collins. He knew she was tired from scrubbing Mr. Cavendish's oven and helping him rewire the lights in their bathroom. But even with Watt and Hank bothering him at school, John was starting to like living

124

with Abigail. No day was ever the same. On her first bus ride to Safe Haven, Abigail dropped old silver buttons in the coin box because they looked like quarters. On her first trip to the bank, Abigail couldn't understand why the bank teller kept asking for her ID.

"I just explained who I am," Abigail told John when he tried to help. "I identified myself quite clearly."

One day, while John was finishing his homework, a pancake slapped him in the face. "My apologies, John Tomas," Abigail said as another pancake flew towards the living room. "Watch your head, Penny! Oops!"

John even started to look forward to some things at school. "As part of our ocean unit," Mrs. Sok told her class one day, "we are going to take a field trip with the fifth graders. Please stop making faces, Watt, and sit up. Daphne Davis is going to talk about some of the creatures that live in the ocean, just as she does on her television program. Keep your hands in your pockets, Watt, if you can't stop pulling Katie's hair. This is a very exciting opportunity for us to learn about Beckon Bay."

Down the hall, Mr. Keenes told Penny's class about the field trip, too. "Apparently, we're entertaining the second graders, so let the little kids hold the compasses and do all the writing. Just make sure they don't tear off the crabs' legs or whatever else we're going to look at. And we're supposed to have extra chaperones for boat trips, so try to get your parents to come along." Mr. Keenes glanced at Penny. "That is, if you've got any parents. Now, Tony, you can pass out the homework."

"I don't think you should come," John told Abigail that night as they cooked dinner. "People won't understand if you do magic by accident. Plus, we're spending the entire time on a ferry. You'll get sick."

"Mrs. LaFontaine said the boat is too big for me to be ill." Abigail counted how many times Penny stirred to mix tomatoes into a pan of black beans. "Mrs. LaFontaine called the Magic Shop specifically to invite me. And I can try to make a special tonic to help with seasickness. I would like to go. It is rare that both your classes are going on the same trip."

"I bet the principal asked you because she wants you to keep an eye on us." Penny pointed Abigail to a plate of chopped cilantro. "Mrs. LaFontaine probably thinks we're going to cause trouble."

"But we're not going to."

"As long as those kids stay out of my way, I'm not doing anything."

"We will be too busy to have trouble." Abigail sprinkled cilantro over the beans with a frown of concentration. "We are going to learn how to read a compass. Daphne Davis will talk about sea animals. How much trouble can that be?"

Two Discoveries

Penny and John each had trouble the moment they stepped on the boat for the field trip.

"Hey, lady!" Hank shouted down from the upper deck. "You in the green gloves – why don't you turn me into a frog? Or a sea turtle?"

"Are you scared to do anything without your babysitter, Henny-Penny?" Caitlin turned to the girls in Penny's class. "The new girl must need a handler."

"Where's your flying carpet, lady?" Watt called down. "Did you take it to the cleaners?"

Watt stood up on the railings. "Look at me! I'm flying, hands free! I don't even need a broom!"

The girls twittered. "Tony's brother is so funny," Caitlin said. "Remember last year when his friend said they had a robot living in their basement?"

"Look at me, Watt! I can fly, too!" But Hank fell backwards as soon as he let go of the rail.

"You boys, come down from there." Mrs. Sok hobbled out of the galley. "And keep your fingers out of your nose, Watt. The presentation will start once the boat leaves the pier."

At that, the deck began to tremble. The motor rumbled and the crew hurried to pull all the lines onto the deck.

Abigail clutched John's hand. "Perhaps this was not such a good idea."

"John, put this rubber band on your guardian's wrist." Mrs. LaFontaine paused as she shepherded fifth graders to the lower deck. "Snap the rubber band and it should ease some of her symptoms. Move along, everyone. Daphne Davis will lecture from the bow."

Kids jostled one another to the front of the boat. They pushed to get closest to the fish tanks at the railings. But Abigail sank onto the first bench she saw. John gave her his baseball cap and Penny handed her a bottle of water. "Thank you, Penelope Rose." Abigail closed her eyes. "I will be fine once the boat stops moving. Do you think we will go back early? Perhaps it will rain."

John scanned the sky for clouds, but all he could see was blue. "I don't think it'll rain."

A low, sparkling laugh made them all turn around. "You can't possibly hope for a better day," Mrs. Davis said. "How do you do – Abigail, isn't it? How are things at the Magic Shop?"

"Wonderful." Abigail swallowed as the boat lurched. "Oh, no."

Penny shook her head. "You're going to be seasick the whole time."

"Mrs. Davis, you've got to start!" Katie ran up and tugged at her sleeve. "Mrs. Sok says you'd better get talking before Watt takes everything out of the fish tank. He and Hank already tried to play catch with a sea urchin."

"Be careful of my sweater – yes, thank you. I will go get my things." Mrs. Davis pried Katie's hand off her arm. "Excuse me, Abigail. I hope you feel better."

Mrs. LaFontaine clapped to get the students' attention. She tried to talk about the experiments John's class had done with magnets. She tried to summarize the research Penny's class had done on sea animals. Nobody listened until Mrs. Davis lifted a horseshoe crab out of the first tank.

She handed the horseshoe crab to Watt. She gave Caitlin a giant starfish. Everyone quieted down to hear Hank list some differences between the two creatures. Everyone raised their hands to guess where they would live in the ocean. When Mrs. Davis smiled, everyone smiled as if they were on her television show – everyone except Abigail, Penny and John.

"Oh, dear," Abigail said, snapping the rubber band again and again. "I thought the tonic would help. Perhaps I should have made it stronger."

"You're going to throw up," John said.

"You'd better lie down." Penny stood up so Abigail could stretch out on the bench.

"Does the new girl know everything?" Mr. Keenes asked over the heads of the students. "That must be why you weren't paying attention. Why don't you tell us what Mrs. Davis was going to say about the lobster Tony's holding?"

"Fine." Penny glared at Mr. Keenes. "That lobster is female. I can tell because she doesn't have one oversized claw. Also she has weak little legs in the middle. You could check to see if a lobsterman cut a notch in her tail. That would mean that she'd been caught once with a lot of eggs on her. And Tony shouldn't be holding her in the first place. The lobster's as long as his arm. That means she's too big to be sold. She should be put back in the ocean." Penny crossed her arms.

"Well said, Penny." Mrs. LaFontaine nodded at her.

"I couldn't have put it better myself," Mrs. Davis said.

But Mr. Keenes was talking with Caitlin about baseball, so he hadn't noticed at all.

Mrs. Sok limped forward. "The first activity is about the animals' habitats. Watt, please don't use the crab as a weapon. Now that the boat has dropped its anchor, all fifth graders should find a partner from the second grade. Second graders, please come to me for the worksheets."

"It's just like being on *Daphne Davis Tames the Wild*," Hank told Watt as they took a compass to the upper deck. "Maybe if we find something important, she'll have us on TV."

"I found a deserted island last summer." Watt pointed to a tiny cluster of rocks topped by a single pine tree. "I saw fairies there and everything. I could tell her all about it."

129

John walked past them with the activity materials. He was glad Watt and Hank had forgotten about Abigail. Everyone had. Sailboats splashed through the water with rainbow-colored spinnakers flying. Cormorants ducked under the waves for fish. The wind smelled like salt and summer. It felt great to be out of school.

"There's Mr. Cavendish." Penny pointed the *Caddy* out to John. Squint sat on the bow with his nose into the wind. "They must have started late. Look, Caddy's screaming at him. Mr. Cavendish should be halfway to town by now."

John held up the compass and waited for the needle to stop wobbling. "Squint's at 20 degrees north."

"It looks like he found the next buoy. See – there's Bill coming to check."

After they watched Mr. Cavendish crank up the first lobster pot, Penny and John took turns filling in the worksheet for Mrs. Davis. From the starboard side of the boat, they wrote the compass bearings to the lighthouse. From the port side, they found the bearings to Watt's deserted island with the one tree. They estimated their location on the chart and marked Mr. Cavendish's beach. John tried to check their answer with one more measurement when he noticed something strange.

"The old fort is supposed to be due north, isn't it? Only the compass has gone all funny. It's pointing in the wrong direction."

"That's right." Mrs. Davis turned away from Caitlin's group. "You're absolutely right. Tell me your name."

"John."

"And Penny is the expert on lobsters. You're both doing well today. Just now, you noticed something unusual." Mrs. Davis pointed to the chart at the bottom of the worksheet. "You see Safe Haven here and the islands there in green? The chart uses darker blues to show where the water is deeper."

"And the numbers tell you how deep the water is," Penny said. "We know. If the water is too shallow, the boat would hit the rocks."

"And here it says 'magnetic disturbance.' There's a deposit of magnetic rocks about where we are now. Do you know why that might affect your compass, John?"

"The magnet in the compass is pulling to the rocks." John checked his compass again. The needle swung back and forth as the boat bobbed in the water. "It's not going to the North Pole like normal."

"That's right. Luckily, this doesn't happen very often. If it did, any sailor relying on a compass would keep losing his way."

"Hey, Mrs. Davis!" Watt poked his head around the galley door. "We saw a couple of seals, right off the back of the boat. They talked to us and everything!"

"Did they really?" Mrs. Davis went to find out. But John turned to Penny.

"Did you hear what she said? Around here, the sailors would lose their way. They lose their direction." He tugged at her arm. "It's like the painting. 'Find three in the sea where you lose your direction.' What if this is it? What if we found one of the hiding places for Abigail's stones?"

Penny looked up at their house, just visible over a cluster of pine trees. "We're not far from home. That Evie witch could have rowed out here without any trouble."

John leaned over the railing. "I can't see anything in the water."

"It can't be that deep. We're close to shore."

"Hey, Penny!"

Penny glanced over her shoulder. She jumped back before a lobster could pinch her nose with its claws.

"You aren't scared of a little lobster, are you?" Tony waved the lobster closer to her face.

Penny knocked it away. "Put it back," she said. "Lobsters shouldn't be out of the water for long."

"I see something!" John stood up on the railing. In the water, he could see the dark outlines of a boulder.

"You put the lobster back if you're so worried, Henny-Penny." Tony threw the lobster at Penny's face.

The lobster flew at Penny, Penny jumped back against John, and the boat suddenly dipped towards the water.

And John tumbled in.

Two Dips in the Ocean

The ocean swallowed John into a wave. Cold seeped through his clothes. John tried to swim towards the sunshine, but he couldn't kick hard enough. Down he sank, deeper into the icy dark. As the light faded above him, a black boulder reached out underneath him. In the darkness, something glinted.

"John!" Penny screamed from the deck of the boat. She didn't pay any attention to the voices yelling behind her. She shook off the hands that tried to hold her back. Penny climbed over the railing and jumped after her brother.

John didn't hear the splash as Penny hit the water. He didn't see her dive after him. His chest felt tight and he needed to breathe. He was drowning, but he kept sinking deeper. A swish of a wave gave him a breath of air for a moment. Another pushed him against a smooth, slick back. He must be dying, John thought while the back lifted him up and up.

Penny dove. She kicked her way to the surface, gasped deeply, and dove again. Mr. Keenes jumped off the boat and tried to grab her, but Penny kicked him away. She dove again and again until, sputtering at the surface, she saw a whiskered nose. The nose poked out of a wave and vanished. When the wave moved on, she saw John resting on the back of a seal.

The crowd on deck cheered.

"No way!" Hank whooped out of excitement. "Did you see him? He rode that seal! That's awesome!"

"He was dead." Watt pushed his way forward. "He was dead when he fell off the boat. That seal brought him back to life by feeding him oxygen. Didn't you see it? The new kid'll be part seal now. He won't eat anything but live fish after this."

"That's enough, Watt," Mrs. Sok said.

"Stand back, everyone, and let John aboard," Mrs. LaFontaine said.

"I'm fine," John told the crew as they hoisted him onto the deck. His legs felt wobbly, but even in the wind, he didn't feel cold or breathless.

"What was it like?" Hank demanded. "Was it hard to hold onto the seal?"

"Of course it wasn't, now that he's part seal." Watt pushed his way over. "What's that in your hand?"

"It's just an old bottle." Hank adjusted his glasses. "Why'd you go after a yellow bottle?"

"There are some rocks in it," Watt said. "They're green. Emeralds, I bet. They're presents from the seal."

133

"I want to see!"

"That's enough now," Mrs. LaFontaine said. "Mrs. Davis, don't let any water ruin that lovely skirt of yours. Perhaps you can tell us about sea mammals in the galley while John dries off. Come along, boys and girls."

"I want to see the stones," Hank protested.

Mrs. Sok held a towel out for John. "Why don't I hold the bottle for you?

John wriggled himself away from everyone. "I have to find Abigail."

John caught sight of her at the bow of the boat, away from everyone else. Clinging to the railing, she looked greener than ever. But over the wind, he heard her sing something down to the seal. John didn't understand the words, but the seal did. The seal barked a deep, jolly bark and dipped its head into the water. With an arch of its back, it slipped below the surface.

"Abigail," John said. He held out the bottle.

Abigail turned and sighed in relief. "You are not hurt in any way, John Tomas? Everything happened so quickly and you were gone for a long time. Perhaps we should sit down." Abigail sank down onto the deck.

"I'm not even cold," John said. "And look what I found. It was right in the water, right where the clue said. See in the bottle? Three stones of green from the ocean."

It took a moment for Abigail to realize what he held out to her. "Three stones from the ocean," she repeated. "How did you —"

"They're smithsonite. I'd bet anything they are." John pulled her to her feet so she could take the bottle. "Hold out your hand."

Flushing an ugly shade of greenish pink, Abigail fingered the stones John poured out of the bottle. Each had been polished smooth and flat on five sides, like the black stones in the attic. "You figured out the next clue – how is it possible? I was starting to think –" She stopped. "Is that why – no, John Tomas, there was no need to put yourself in danger – and for Squint – What if you had injured yourself as you fell in?"

"Falling in was an accident." John grinned. "But it was a lucky accident, too, don't you think? Now you have the green stones you need."

Abigail pocketed the stones so she could hug him. "That I do."

They watched the crew tug Penny up and out of the water. Mr. Keenes was yelling about how stupid she'd been to jump overboard, but Penny didn't listen. She didn't wait for Mrs. Sok to hand her a towel. As soon as she got on board, she went right up to Abigail and held out her hand. It quivered and her voice shook. "Thank you," Penny said.

Abigail nearly hugged her, too, but then the captain started the motor for the ride back home. "Oh, dear," Abigail said, holding her stomach again.

Penny turned to John. "And you're ok?"

"I'm fine," he said. Salt-crusted and wet, John felt better than fine.

Two Treats

When John climbed into bed that evening, he thought that they were done with adventures, at least for a little while. But after they had brushed their teeth and picked out books to read, Squint leaped into their bedroom with a yowl of announcement. Abigail followed and held her arms out wide.

"Magic just brought us bicycles – one for each of us!"

Penny put aside her book. "You can't take bikes instead of a salary," she reminded her. "Most of the money from Social Services had to pay the oil bill. We won't have anything for groceries."

"I promise I will ask Magic about money tomorrow." Abigail plopped Squint on her bed before he started playing with the hole in John's sneaker. "But tonight, we must test the bicycles out. Magic suggested we ride down the road for ice cream. I have never had ice cream before. For that matter, I have never ridden a bicycle either. It will be fun."

"We're in our pajamas," John said.

"Of course you are. All my books say you ought to wear pajamas at night." Abigail sat beside him on the bed. "On the other hand, my books also say you should go to bed early."

"Your books are wrong about that." Penny reached for her sneakers. "The sun hasn't even set yet. Anyway, we should do something to celebrate. John nearly drowned today."

"Hurrah!" John jumped up on his bed. "I love ice cream. I'm going to get a sugar cone with chocolate ice cream and chocolate cookies." He fell back on the mattress and jumped up again. "With chocolate sprinkles!"

"I have never had ice cream before." Abigail bounced into the air as he jumped. "Perhaps I will try vanilla – and pineapple – and pumpkin pie!"

John began to laugh. "Fried chicken, too."

"And Penelope Rose will have tomato and sweet corn and coconut!"

"And pizza!"

Abigail slid onto the floor with a bump. "Do they make pizza ice cream?"

John tugged Abigail to her feet. "Pizza ice cream would be gross," he said. "But it would be funny, too."

Penny thought they looked pretty funny as they climbed on the bicycles. John had a rusty man's bike that was too big for him. She had a little girl's bike with dirty tassels and an old basket. But Abigail's bicycle was the strangest.

"I've never seen a grown-up with training wheels," John said.

"Or wearing a purple helmet covered in stars," Penny said. "Abigail, do you have to stuff your skirt in your socks? It looks weird."

"All my books say that bicycle safety is key." Abigail honked her horn as she rolled down the driveway, her knees bent to her elbows. "Now, really, this is not difficult at all."

137

John pumped hard to zoom down the driveway and onto the street. "Follow me!"

"Mrrow!" Squint sprang into Penny's basket.

"We'll race you." Penny stood up to pedal fast.

Abigail squeezed her horn again. "And I will win!"

Two Battles Won

With John leading the way, Penny and Abigail coasted down hills that led away from the seashore and alongside the strawberry field. They pedaled past summer cottages glowing blue with the light from television sets. Cars drove by sleepily and people yawned as they walked their dogs. But John got a burst of energy when he saw the line of kids standing in front of the ice cream stand.

"We found it!" He threw his bicycle down on the gravel and ran to order. Squint hopped to the ground before Penny stopped her bike. Abigail hustled after him. Penny held back, though, wishing she were home in bed. Most of her class from school had reassembled on one of the picnic tables. As long as they didn't turn around –

"Look at you." A wad of chewed-up cigar landed at Penny's feet. In the shadows of a dumpster, perched on an old motorcycle, Mal pushed back her hat. "Still together, I see. How is the job search going?"

"Fine." Penny tried to keep her voice low.

"Your guardian never found work, did she? Nothing has burned down in over a week."

"She got a job in town." Penny checked over her shoulder. None of the kids from her class were paying attention. "Sorry, Mal, but Abigail's waiting for me to order."

138

Mal waved her away without another word. But just as Penny reached the head of the line, Mal bellowed across the parking lot, "I recommend the fresh strawberry and white chocolate, young lady!"

Penny winced.

"Hey, it's Henny-Penny." Tony pointed his ice cream cone at her. "Nice outfit, new girl."

Penny tried to ignore him, but Tony didn't stop. "Look! It's the lady from the field trip. She's got an entire solar system on her head!" Tony counted eight planets and four comets on Abigail's helmet. "And doesn't she ever take her gloves off?"

"Maybe she'll get seasick again." Penny heard Caitlin laugh. "She can hardly walk with her skirt tucked in like that. Look at those socks!"

"How much ice cream did she order?"

"She must have gotten one of every flavor."

"There are seven scoops on her cone."

"Nine, I think."

"What a pig."

Just then, just when all the kids were watching, Abigail's nose hit her tower of ice cream. One – two – three scoops of ice cream tumbled down the front of her skirt. With a wet thump, they plopped on the ground.

"Oh," Abigail said.

"Ha-ha!" Tony pointed so everyone would see. "She doesn't even know how to eat ice cream."

The girls giggled.

"She was useless on the boat," Caitlin said, "and she's worse on land. Can't she do anything right?"

John turned his back on them. "Here." He held his cone out to Abigail. "Take my ice cream. I just remembered. I don't like chocolate."

"No, thank you, John Tomas." Abigail tossed her empty cone into the dumpster. "You enjoy yourself. This is a lesson for me not to be so greedy."

"We can get you another one," Penny said.

Abigail shook her head. "Not until Magic pays me. We just spent all the money left over from the water bill."

"She's going to cry!" Caitlin's voice carried across the picnic tables.

Tony made fake crying noises. "She lost her ice cream. Boo-hoo!"

Abigail's eyes had begun to shimmer, but she forced out a laugh. "Come now, Penelope Rose. Please do not let my foolishness spoil the evening."

"It's already ruined," Penny said. "Those kids can say what they want about me, but it's not fair to go after you."

"Be careful now." Mal settled herself back in her seat and waved a new cigar at an old station wagon. "Here comes that woman with the nose. She will not be happy to see you."

"I don't care." Penny was too angry to hear any warnings about Mrs. Collins. She was too mad to be careful. Abigail had saved John – how dare they say anything – if the kids in Penny's class thought they could pick on Abigail and get away with it – Penny was so mad that she stomped to the top of the nearest picnic table. She marched across the neighboring picnic tables until she reached Caitlin's.

Caitlin crossed her arms. "What do you want?"

Tony climbed onto the table to look Penny in the eye. "Yeah, what?"

"I want you to leave our guardian alone. She never did anything to you."

140

Tony sniggered. "What'd she do for you? Choose your clothes?"

"We're really jealous." Caitlin used her sweetest voice. "Did she find those bikes in the dump?"

"She must have," Tony said. "My brother Herbert said she didn't have money when she went to Mal's. He said you had to work for groceries."

"And didn't she set the Clam Shack on fire?" Caitlin giggled.

"She can't do anything right, can she, Henny-Penny?"

"What would you know?" Penny shoved Tony's shoulder so hard he stumbled. "Abigail's learning. She's getting better every day, but you wouldn't understand." Penny shoved him again. "You don't try anything you've never done before. You wouldn't. You'd be too scared you'd look dumb." With one last shove, Tony slipped off the end of the picnic table and slammed flat on his back in the dirt.

"You do look dumb," Penny said. "You'll never know how much courage it takes for Abigail to be here."

"You got ice cream in my hair!" Caitlin screamed. "And all over my new dress." Caitlin jumped up on the table and swung her hand. But before she could slap Penny, a puff of air swept her off her feet and face down into someone's sundae. Tony tried to get to his feet, but Squint got in the way.

"Srrow." Squint flicked his tail in Tony's face.

The other kids started shouting. Squint leaped to the top of the table and stretched out his claws. Two of the kids went to tackle Penny. The wind rose.

"Hold it right there, Missy." Mrs. Collins slammed her car door so loudly all the kids jumped back. "I

141

knew you'd cause me another headache. Tonight, my first night off in weeks, I got a craving for some soft serve. All I wanted was a peaceful evening. Then here you are, picking another fight. Are you trying to get locked up, Missy? Do you want me to put you in that girl's home?"

Squint hissed. The wind fell away, discouraged. Penny didn't know what to say. Abigail and John were hurrying over, but they wouldn't be able to do anything either. Penny knew she was in trouble.

"Ha! Ha! Ha!" Laughing more to break the tension, a man climbed out of a sports car. "I hate to interrupt, but I did witness the whole thing." He walked into the light looking more as if he'd stepped out of a magazine cover. "It's funny, actually."

"Wow," Caitlin said.

"You're Trey Davis." Tony couldn't believe his eyes. "You're on tv."

"You're a millionaire." Mrs. Collins touched her hair. "A million times over."

"Ha, ha, ha!" Mr. Davis didn't laugh from his belly the way he would if something were really funny. His smile came too quickly. "Nobody is a millionaire a million times over. Ha! How do you do? I'm Trey Davis. What a gorgeous night for soft serve."

"It's gorgeous." Mrs. Collins stared at his hand. "Oh, yes, you are. I mean, it's gorgeous ice cream. I mean, it's a nice soft serve." Mrs. Collins almost giggled, but it turned into a snort. "You have a great smile."

"Wow," Caitlin said again.

Penny rolled her eyes, but stopped when Mr. Davis noticed. "We're just leaving," she said.

"What about your cat?"

"My cat?" Penny glanced down. Squint winked up at her. "I guess he was just getting started."

"Mrrow," said Squint.

"Ha!" Mr. Davis offered an arm to help her climb off the table. "You're a valiant defender when your temper is up. Missy, is it?"

"Penny."

"Your guardian ought to be proud of you."

Everyone looked at Abigail, ice cream-covered and hobbled by her skirt. She waved, but then her helmet fell over her eyes.

Mr. Davis cleared his throat. "Of course, in my experience, Penny, a lady tames more tigers with a firm voice than she does with a whip. I'd suggest that you'd make your point better without scuffling in a parking lot." Mr. Davis offered Caitlin his handkerchief. "And you would keep more ice cream out of your hair."

Caitlin blushed as she wiped a dribble from her ear. The people eavesdropping at nearby tables nodded in agreement. Mr. Davis smiled at them, too.

"Ice cream," Mrs. Collins said, still in a daze.

Mr. Davis put an arm around Tony's shoulder. "You should know better than to fight young ladies, especially when this ice cream stand is just trying to run its business. How about you wipe the mess off the table while I treat this kind woman here to a soft serve wafer cone. Vanilla?"

"Vanilla," Mrs. Collins repeated.

Mr. Davis gave Penny another bow and led Mrs. Collins to place her order. The other kids stared after them.

Penny rolled her eyes. "Let's go," she told Squint.

John followed her to their bicycles. "I thought the Wart Hog was going to get you for sure."

"Me too."

"And I as well." Abigail fiddled with the bell on her bicycle. "My books speak firmly against fighting, Penelope Rose. Mr. Davis is correct. Perhaps we should discuss a better way of resolving conflicts."

"We should have a talk." Penny grinned. "You didn't have to blow Caitlin into a bowl of whipped cream face first. You could have left her to me."

"Or me," John said.

"Mrrow," Squint said as he leaped into Penny's basket.

"That's right." Penny adjusted her helmet. "From now on, they'd better watch out. Nobody picks on our family and gets away with it."

"Huh." Squint ducked to avoid another wad of chewed-up cigar. Mal grunted as she took a paper bag from her fender. "You folks manage to get yourselves in and out of trouble better than anyone I have ever seen. Here. You might as well take this home."

Startled, Penny peeked inside the bag. She looked up, confused. "You shouldn't give us your ice cream."

"Really, Mal, please," Abigail said.

"Don't you want it yourself?" John asked.

"You will enjoy it more." Mal leaned forward and with a rumble, kicked her motorcycle on. "But in return, young man, do me a favor. Keep out of trouble for a few weeks. Try enjoying this new family for awhile. You may be surprised how much you like it." With a sputter of gravel, Mal rode down the dark street. "See you around."

"Bye," John called after her.

"That was surprising," Abigail said.

"Hrrow." Squint sniffed at the bag.

"I agree," Abigail said. "Let us go home."

144

"Yeah." Penny almost reached over to give her a hug.

Two Tales of Things Lost and Found

As summer vacation approached, Penny and John had more work to do on weekends than they ever did during the school week. On Saturday mornings, they woke up in moonlight in order to be out on the *Caddy* before sunrise. As the day started, John worked on deck alongside Mr. Cavendish hauling up traps. They tossed lobsters back into the ocean or into the tank that stood near the cockpit. Then John flung old bait up to Bill and Burt, dropped new pieces of fish guts back into the traps and dragged the traps to Mr. Cavendish to tip back into the water. Mr. Cavendish kept his eye on Penny at the helm, but Squint, sitting up on the bow, was the one who gave her directions whenever another boat came their way. Caddy flew overhead to see where they had to motor for the next trap and they all took turns to radio the harbor when they were ready to dock. After a few trips, John had become used to smelling like fish. Penny didn't notice anymore the crusty, dry feeling of salt on her skin.

If they docked in Safe Haven early, Penny and John sat on the deck while Mr. Cavendish sold his catch. Sometimes, they looked for The Trader to ask him about the stopper, but his shop was always locked tight. Sometimes, Penny drew pictures of the harbor while

John made up stories. Most of the time, they visited Abigail at work and ate sandwiches with Magic. On rare occasions, when the ocean was very calm, Abigail drank the strongest tonic she could stomach and climbed aboard the *Caddy* when it was time to ride home.

"Hey, Mr. Cavendish," John said one Saturday in June. "Do you know any pirate stories? Abigail said you would."

"I did," Abigail said, wiggling her toes off the side of the boat. "Mr. Cavendish, I thought you would be an expert."

Mr. Cavendish pulled on his nose. "Don't know about that," he said.

"There weren't pirates in Maine, were there?" Penny waved at Mr. Davis, skippering a new yacht.

John flicked a finger full of fish guts at her. "I bet there are stories."

"Stories?" Mr. Cavendish took the wheel and sent Penny to help fill bags with fresh bait. "I guess there are stories. Heard plenty of stories about the littlest island out there."

"Which one?" Abigail counted four scattered across the bay.

"Hope Island." Penny pointed to it with a gooey finger. "The tiny one with the single tree."

John got a bucket to wash down the deck. "One of the boys at school said he saw fairies there."

"You're kidding," Penny said. "I bet that was Watt. He's always making stuff up."

"All kinds of fairy stories about Hope Island," Mr. Cavendish said, turning towards home. "Odd-shaped holes dug around tree roots. Funny sounds around the new moon."

147

"You know, we might have a painting of Hope Island in the living room," Abigail said. "What do you think, John Tomas?"

"Might be." Mr. Cavendish squinted into the sun. "It's real picturesque out there. Kind of sad, too. Knew someone who went out there for the moonlight once. She never came back."

"Evie," John realized.

"That's who you were talking about," Penny said. "That's the girl you lost. She's why you knew how to help Abigail and Squint – and why you never got married."

"Why I went away," Mr. Cavendish said. "Why I came back in the end. There's no place like our harbor here." He nodded toward the lighthouse, white and proud overlooking the green islands. "The Headlight has the best view of all. Catches every sunrise, every sunset, and all the storms in between." He pulled on his nose. "No telling what odd thing it's seen here in the harbor."

"Like what?" John and Penny sat back to listen. Abigail looked up.

Mr. Cavendish shaded his eyes as he looked out over the water. "One of my first nights lobstering, I was out with Caddy. Fog came up, thickest fog I'd ever seen. Couldn't hardly see the water over the side of the boat. All I could hear was the bell on the buoy out there and the horn from the Headlight. Tried to keep each one on opposite sides of the boat and hoped I'd find my way. Caddy called out if I went off course and we found the mooring eventually. But when I went to tie up, right there, I saw a face looking up out of the water at me."

"Really?"

"What was it?"

"Was it a ghost?"

"Was it a whale?"

"Or a seal?"

"Were you scared?"

"What was it?"

"Don't know what it was." Mr. Cavendish slowed the motor down. "Hop up there, John. You're back on duty."

John clambered over Abigail to grab the mooring, but he was still listening.

"Wasn't big enough to be a whale," Mr. Cavendish said. "Didn't look dark or hairy or shiny enough to be anything else. My grandfather always said there were spirits out here in the water. I'd venture a guess that he was right."

Penny shivered. John pulled the line up on board and waited for Squint to tell him he'd knotted it correctly. Then he asked for another story. "One about pirates. You have to know one about pirates."

"Can't say that I know anything about pirates." He nodded at Abigail, tying the laces of her blue boots. "But your guardian there spoke to me about an outing this afternoon. Sort of treasure hunt."

John swung back onto the deck. "Really? A real treasure hunt?"

"For this time of year it is," Mr. Cavendish said. "It's funny for early June."

Abigail knew what John was thinking. "It may not be a real treasure, but there is hunting involved."

Penny straightened up from stowing away the gear. "Didn't you say you needed us to paint your front steps? We owe you for putting new pipes in the bathroom."

Mr. Cavendish gave Abigail a hand into the dinghy before offering one to Penny. "You get me some treasure this afternoon and we'll call it even," he said.

Two Treasure Hunts

They wouldn't find the treasure on the beach, Abigail said. They hoisted themselves into Mr. Cavendish's truck and bounced over potholes and past Postman's Hack. They wouldn't find the treasure at home either, she said. Finally, when Mr. Cavendish pulled into a dirt road in the middle of a field, Abigail said they'd struck gold.

"Strawberries!" Abigail slammed the truck door with a flourish. "Fresh strawberries growing right here! I saw them from the bus yesterday."

"Yum!" John scrambled off the back of the trunk and grabbed a green container from the farm stand.

Penny stood up in the truck bed and shaded her eyes to look out over the field. Away from the water, the light flattened out the colors on the field. She didn't see any strawberries, just short, dusty plants. "It's early for strawberries, isn't it?"

"But they are here." Abigail's long skirt flapped as she strode up and over the rows. She swung her arms around and looked back at Penny. "This is just what it smells like in my valley in Umbra. It is all strawberries and sunshine and earth and evergreens."

Penny swung herself off truck. "So you know how to pick strawberries?"

"Of course." Abigail knelt down. "Our berries grow on hillsides, so they stay as small as diamonds. But here – look, Penelope Rose – see, they are as long as my finger!"

150

The strawberries dangled fat and low to the ground under emerald leaves. Penny worked quickly, John worked quietly and Abigail exclaimed every time she saw a flash of red. She also cried out when she nearly stumbled over someone.

"Mal, what a surprise it is to see you here!" Abigail said. "But then we should have guessed. Are you gathering berries for your market?"

Mal put her hands on her hips. She wore a squashed, broad hat that seemed to be nearly as big as she was. "I have no idea," she said. "Most of these berries would not meet customers' standards."

"Really?" Abigail held a strawberry up, scarlet and dappled with tiny, golden seeds. "I think they are gorgeous."

"Your standards are low." Mal poked John's arm. "Juicy – sweet – unbruised – that is what you want, young man. Ignore the dirt or mosquitoes." Mal pushed aside berries that had already darkened and missed their prime. She disregarded berries that were not ripe enough to fall into her hand. But in a moment, she'd filled half his carton.

"No need to thank me," Mal told him as she strode away. "I have been doing this much longer than you have."

It didn't take Penny long to feel like she'd been picking strawberries for hours. The field smelled like hot strawberry jam and Penny felt like hot melted butter was rolling down the back of her neck. She thought about mint ice cream and lemonade and sitting in an air-conditioned room drawing pictures of pirates. She thought about cherry popsicles and raspberry snow cones and splashing through the waves on the beach.

151

There were two more weeks until the last day of school, but Penny wanted a vacation.

"Just a few more baskets," she heard Mr. Cavendish say to John. "And you'll have enough strawberries for a pie tomorrow."

"And ice cream and shortcake and strawberry soup!" John couldn't wait.

Penny kept picking.

John hunched over to find berries the way Mal had shown him. He was walking so carefully, he almost ran into Mrs. Davis at the farm stand.

"Hello, there, John," Mrs. Davis said as she turned off her phone. "How nice it is to see you again. I thought I recognized your sisters out there in the fields."

Penny walked up from behind John to drop off a full carton. "Abigail's not our sister. She's our foster parent."

A few rows away, Abigail clapped her hands. "There is an entire bouquet of berries right here, John Tomas. Come see! They are just like rubies under all that green."

"Wait up!" John jumped over a puddle and ran down to her. "Don't pick them all!"

Mrs. Davis tried not to notice the spots on her white pants. "Oh, don't worry, Penny. I've got another pair at home. And who can blame John for being excited over the first strawberries of the summer. I love anything that tastes so wonderful without cooking."

"You're talking to the wrong person here," Mr. Cavendish said as he put Penny's strawberries in the back of his truck. "Penny and her brother there have spent the last few weeks cooking and cleaning for me and Abigail. Not ones to complain, neither."

Embarrassed, Penny made a face, but Mrs. Davis winked at her. "That's not the first time someone has told me about how hard you're working," she said, "but I suspect you wouldn't mind a day off now and again. Some time when you're free, you can come by our house for a visit. Most of our bathhouse is filled with toy samples for Trey's stores."

Penny's eyes opened wide. "John would love that."

But John didn't hear about the toys. He didn't hear Mrs. Davis describe the hot tub they'd put off the master bath or the putting green they'd planted near the ocean. As he filled another basket, John thought about what Abigail had said. It was a field of rubies.

John scanned the landscape. If he looked towards the ocean, he could just barely see the roof of the lighthouse. When he walked forward, more of the lighthouse appeared. He jogged backwards and saw less. John hopped over a row of plants, stepped forward and back again until the lighthouse seemed to disappear over the hill. He circled around, realizing that he'd have a whole radius to search.

"Are you dancing, young man?" Mal pushed her hat back on her head. "Watch out. You could damage the plants."

Maybe the ground had moved and shifted since Evie's time. Maybe they'd have to dig up the whole field. John ate a strawberry and thought. Figuring out the clue shouldn't be this hard. But each row stretched long and identical with their short, green plants – that is, all of the rows were the same except one. One row had a gap. And as he walked to the gap, the lighthouse appeared to vanish.

John started digging where no strawberries could grow. He dug deeper with both his hands, down and

153

down until one of his fingers jammed against the smooth curve of a bottle. There, in the soft, rich dirt, a purple bottle held three ivory-colored stones.

"What have you got there?" Mal hoisted herself to her feet and tromped over strawberry plants to see.

Abigail looked up, too. "Are you finished picking strawberries?"

John held it out the bottle.

Abigail stared at it for a moment. "You found another bottle,"

John nodded. "Three stones of white from the earth."

"You found them!" Abigail crushed several plants to give him a hug.

"Just two more bottles to go!"

Mal kicked the dirt back into the hole John had dug. "A strawberry field is a funny place for a bottle of rocks."

"But it is like a field of rubies." Abigail patted John's back. "How clever you are, John Tomas."

"You said we were treasure hunting."

Mal tossed away a bruised strawberry. "Pretty worthless treasure, I would think. Here – " She held out her hand. "Give me a look at them."

"You will not want to get your hands dirty, Mal." Abigail tucked the bottle in a pocket of her skirt. "We would hate to trouble you after all your help today. What do you think, John Tomas? We have another reason to celebrate. Have we picked enough strawberries to make a pie?"

"I think yes," John said firmly. "Strawberry pie with whipped cream."

"I will need Penelope Rose for help with whipped cream." Abigail kissed the top of his head. "Have a good day, Mal."

Mal pulled her hat further down on her head. "Sure," she said. She sounded grouchy.

At the other corner of the field, Mrs. Davis paid for her strawberries and turned to Penny. "I'm filming humpback whales in a few weeks, but perhaps we can have you over beforehand. It's about time that we had some children to treat. Do enjoy your time with them, Mr. Cavendish."

"Lovely lady, that," Mr. Cavendish commented as Mrs. Davis drove away. "Husband's just the same. As easy-going as you come, but not a hair out of place. Quite a house they're building behind my place. She practically has a zoo in her back yard." Mr. Cavendish lifted a tray of strawberries onto his truck. "We're lucky they decided to move here."

Penny didn't move. She watched the dust sweep up behind Mrs. Davis' car. It settled over Abigail and John walking back through the field. Swinging Abigail's hand, John laughed. Penny looked at them and began to worry.

Two Lessons

Penny woke up before the sun. John was sleeping with his face smashed into his pillow, but outside some sparrows were discussing breakfast. Penny remembered that Sunday mornings used to mean muffins and strawberries. Back when her mother was teaching her how to cook, when John was little and their mother had a job, sunny Sunday mornings were Penny's favorites. Penny pushed back the covers. She would make everyone a treat.

That morning, however, the sun never came out.

"Someone took half of the muffins!" Penny shouted up the stairs. "I made enough for Mr. Cavendish and there are only four left in the oven. John!"

"I didn't take them."

"Squint!"

Looking distracted, Abigail hurried into the kitchen. "I doubt Squint would take so many, Penelope Rose. But did you notice if he has my glove?"

"No." Penny slammed the oven door shut. "But you're going to be late – and so are we. John!"

"I can't find my shoes."

"We're going to be late," Penny repeated.

The rest of the day didn't go much better. A steady drizzle soaked through their clothes. The wet wind chilled their fingers and rubbed their knuckles red. Mr. Cavendish was gruff because he didn't find many lobsters. Bill, Burt and Caddy fought over fish and screamed so loudly even Squint yowled at them to quiet down.

"You kids go get your lunch," Mr. Cavendish said once they reached the dock in Safe Haven. "I'll find you at the Magic Shop when I'm through here. With any luck the sun will be out by then."

But things weren't any better at the Magic Shop. Penny and John arrived at the store to find it filling with waves of paper pouring out of the cash register.

"It was fine when Mal bought that lipstick," Abigail was telling Magic. "And when Mrs. Collins came to speak with you, nothing happened. Then I hit a button and it kept printing. See, look –" She tapped a blue button and the cash register began to shake. It printed out more paper, and then they heard a pop. Suddenly, the machine began to smoke.

"Honey, we've got to stop this before it catches fire –" Poof! Magic and Abigail jumped back as the machine burst into flames.

Magic tore a tapestry from the ceiling. "Call the fire department!"

"Yes, of course." Abigail turned to the window and called, "Fire department!"

The flames trickled along the stream of paper and lapped at the tapestry Magic kept hitting against the cash register. With a clang, the fire alarm shook the windows. Sprinklers in the ceiling showered foam over the store. Abigail began to cough, Magic began to sputter, and Penny pushed them both out of the way.

Diving beneath the stream of paper, she tugged out the plug for the cash register. John found the phone in the corner and told the fire department what happened. As he hung up, Magic beat the last flame away from the register and stomped out the last cinders. Then she surveyed her store.

Every rack of clothes was covered in frothy white foam. Curls of paper covered the floor. All together, it looked as if a blizzard had swept through the shop. Penny looked at John, wearing a cone of foam on his head. John looked at Penny, half-buried in the sea of paper. Magic looked at them both, but then she caught sight of herself in a mirror. Smudged with smoke and dribbling with foam, she burst out laughing. "Is this a soap factory?"

Penny climbed to her feet. "You aren't mad?" she asked.

Magic laughed harder than ever. "Look at you," she said, holding her sides. "You poor old thing – your hair is turning white fifty years early."

"But your store –" John said.

Magic pointed at him. "You look like a shorn little lamb." She laughed even more.

"I am so terribly sorry," Abigail said.

"None of that, my dear." Magic mopped tears and foam from her eyes with a handful of paper. "I thought I'd seen everything, but never something like this."

"Is Abigail going to lose her job?" John asked.

"She did the last time there was a fire," Penny said.

"No, sugar plum, of course she's not losing her job." Magic gave Abigail's hand a squeeze. "It's worth more than a whole day's business to have a laugh like that. Besides, something good can come out of any mistake. We were planning on scrubbing the store down next week and now, half the work is done."

Penny looked around the shop. "Do you need help cleaning up?"

With a waft of smoke, the cash register popped open, charred and melted. With a wail, the smoke detector went off. Foam shot out from the ceiling again. Outside, they could hear the whine of sirens.

Mal wiped the foam off Penny's head. "Sweet pea, no, you go have fun somewhere while we deal with the fire department."

Abigail sighed. "You may as well go back to Mr. Cavendish. Do you need lunch?"

"We've got muffins." Penny dug into her backpack and pulled out a tin. "I'll leave some for you. You'll need them."

"See, cookie, you don't have to worry about your ducklings. These two can take care of themselves." Chuckling, Magic went to hold the door open for Penny and John, but she slipped and fell into a pile of foam.

Penny and John could hear her laughing all the way down the street to the pier.

Two Puzzles

The drizzle hung thick in the air when Penny and John returned to the *Caddy*. Far away, the lighthouse warned of fog. Under the pier, Bill squawked as Burt picked at a dead fish in the water.

"Yuck." John couldn't watch.

"Seagulls will eat anything," Penny said. "Burt, you're going to be sick."

159

"Hey." John pointed. At the end of the pier glowed the soft light of a lantern. "The Trader must have come back."

"It's about time." Penny stood up. "He's got some questions to answer about that stopper."

John thought so, too. "None of the other bottles had anything like it. The yellow bottle just had a regular cork. The purple one did, too."

"You have them with you, don't you?" Penny picked up the backpack. "Let's see if we can get that stopper back."

A bell jangled as Penny pushed the shop door open. An oil lamp stood beside an ancient cash register. Curtains of cobwebs hid bottles in shadows. The shop appeared empty. Then John looked up.

"Ah." The Trader lounged on a beam over their heads. With a toothpick, he poked spiders out of their cobwebs. "Here you are again. To what do I owe this pleasure? Not another bottle?"

Penny craned her neck. "The stopper," she said. "We want to make a trade with some bottles. John found two more."

"Two more bottles?" The Trader tucked the toothpick behind his ear and swung to the floor. "Finders, seekers, you certainly are the collectors."

"This bottle is bigger than the last one." John set the bottles beside the cash register. "And the color on the yellow bottle is the best of them all."

"It is unusual." The Trader took the bottle between his fingers. In the dim light, the color darkened to gold. "Pretty. Why would you want to trade it away?"

"Why do you want the stopper so much?" Penny asked.

"Ah." The Trader smiled, showing long, yellow teeth. "I am always open to a good trade."

"John's offering you one."

The Trader turned the bottle over in his fingers. "I suppose the bottles were empty when you found them."

"No, but we gave everything to Abigail."

"Of course you did." The Trader placed the bottle back with the other two. "And now you want your stopper."

"We could do the bottle-counting game for it," John suggested.

"I think not." The Trader smiled again. "You are too smart for me now."

"We're not."

"Really?" The Trader popped the toothpick in his mouth. "Then how about this: you complete a puzzle and I will trade."

John had learned to be suspicious. "And if we can't do it?"

"No trade. And no losses." The Trader crouched down and looked up at him. "You may even find this useful."

John bent down with him. "What's the puzzle?"

"It is not an ordinary puzzle." The Trader used his toothpick to draw two designs in the dust on the floor. "Twelve spaces – puzzle pieces, if you like. Put a bottle in each piece."

"But the catch is –" Penny knew the puzzle couldn't be easy.

"The catch is that no piece has a bottle matching the color of any of its neighbors."

"So red can't touch red. Blue can't touch blue."

"Exactly."

Penny shook her head. "You've got about a hundred different colors in here. John could put a different one in each space. What's the challenge?"

The Trader put his toothpick back in his mouth. "The challenge is figuring out the least number of colors you would need."

"And the answer is the same for both of them?"

"Not too hard, is it?" The Trader waved his arm at John. "What do you say, boy-o?"

John considered the map.

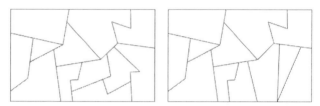

One color wouldn't work. He could see that right away.

"Can you do it with two colors?" Penny muttered to him.

John shook his head. But three colors? John found four blue bottles, four clear bottles, and four green bottles. He tried the three colors on the first design, then on the other. He rearranged the bottles. Most of the first puzzle could be filled with only three colors. It was the same for the second. But each design had a corner that kept messing him up.

"What about five colors?" Penny asked.

"It's four," John said. He turned to The Trader. "I know the answer. It's got to be more than three colors or else the same colors will touch in the bottom corner. Four is the smallest number that you can use. See? It wouldn't even matter what the map looked like. It would still have to be four."

The Trader whistled again. "So it would appear."

"So we can trade?" Penny climbed to her feet.

"Now there is the problem." The Trader chewed on the toothpick. "You see, I already traded the stopper away."

"Hey." John stood up. "You should have told us."

"I just did."

"You said we could trade if John figured out the puzzle." Penny put her hands on her hips. "That was the deal."

"Ah, yes." The Trader leaped back over his counter. "And trade we will. I will trade you any two bottles you like for the two you offered."

Penny put her hands on her hips. "You mean, John can have the big bottle with the ship inside if he wants?"

The Trader reached a long arm over the jar of dead rats. "Here you are."

"And one for Penny." John looked around. "There – that tiny golden jar."

"Ok," Penny said. Swirls of colors melted into the gold in the jar.

"Interesting." The Trader tossed the jar to her. "You both are very interesting."

"We are?" John asked.

"Why?" Penny frowned.

"I am sure many people are interested in what you do." And draping his arms around their shoulders, The Trader led them to the door. "I must bid you farewell for now. But please visit again, particularly if you find anything new. You know now that I am always interested in a trade."

And the door closed firmly behind them.

Two Dinners

Penny and John felt more cheerful that evening. Mr. Cavendish had let John radio the Coast Guard when they passed a buoy with a broken light. He had let Penny steer the entire way back and Squint hadn't interfered once. Dinner that night was Penny's gooiest macaroni and cheese, and by the time Abigail stumbled through the door, Penny and John had made cozy nests on the living room couch.

"What an afternoon." Abigail collapsed on her rocking chair. "If I could have cleaned things my way, the clothes would have washed themselves. It takes hours doing things normally. Magic thinks we will need to work late tomorrow to put everything right again."

On the wall behind them, the clock pinged seven times. The two little men danced out with almost full circles in their little hands. They bonked each other on the head and danced back inside again. Their little doors shut with a click.

Penny headed to the kitchen. "You'll feel better after you eat something."

"And you'll be glad later you did things the ordinary way," John said. "You'll be stronger."

"I am not sure if I care anymore." Abigail sighed.

Squint stretched onto Penny's seat on the sofa. "Mrrow," he said.

"Yes, I know I should not say such things. But I am discouraged, cat, not having had an hour to nap in front of a fire – unlike some buccaneers I know. If you ever did anything truly useful –" Abigail stopped when someone knocked at the door.

"It's Mrs. Davis," Penny called from the kitchen. "I saw her come up the driveway. You'll have to let her in, John. The oven just spilled pasta all over the floor."

"I know you have school tomorrow," Mrs. Davis said as John brought her into the living room. "Still, the weather report is perfect for a barbecue. We're going to host a party for all our neighbors. Please come. A sponsor just sent me a cage full of parakeets and we finally have the pool open. We'd like everyone to be there."

Abigail clapped her hands. "I have never been to a party! How kind of you."

Penny carried out Abigail's dinner and a plate of cookies for Mrs. Davis. "I thought you said you had to work tomorrow night."

"And Mr. Cavendish has the meeting about lobster prices." John pushed Squint over on the couch so Mrs. Davis could sit down. "He won't be able to go either."

"So the two of you were going to be left on your own? All evening?" Mrs. Davis saw all the cat hair on the sofa and chose to stand. "Now you have to join us. I can even pick you up at school. Please say yes. We'd love it."

"Then we'll accept!" John bounced so hard on his seat, Squint complained. "It will be a parakeet pool party."

"I am sure you will have a grand time," Abigail said. "Squint, stop growling. Nobody cares for your opinion."

Mrs. Davis' phone chirped again. "I had better get going. I want to get my nails done before tomorrow."

"We can meet you by the flagpole at school," Penny said.

"For the parakeet pool party!"

165

"You'll have to come to the next barbecue, Abigail." Mrs. Davis held out a hand to her. "We can have another in a few weeks. It would be the perfect time for blueberries then."

"A blueberry barbecue!"

"I will look forward to it." But Abigail's eyes were on the clock. Penny noticed and frowned.

Two Seats at a Table

The ride home from school looked different from the back seat of Mrs. Davis' white convertible. In the bright sunlight, Abigail's gray house seemed withered and crotchety. Mr. Cavendish's cottage looked faded and small. Penny wished she had worn a newer pair of jeans to school. She wished John had worn a clean sweatshirt. Mrs. Davis wore clothes as clean and crisp as the leather in her new car, and her manners were impeccable. She asked Penny the right questions about homework and allergies and things to eat for dinner. She made John laugh at a story about elephants interrupting her breakfast on safari. Mrs. Davis raced June breezes until they were breathless, and then stopped the car in front of a grand mansion overlooking the water.

"Welcome to our home," Mrs. Davis said. "You'll have to excuse the scaffolding in the garden. We're not finished with all the construction."

But Penny and John didn't see a mess when she opened the front door. Everywhere was marble, wood and crystal. African masks hung over Asian vases overflowing with roses. Twelve tiny birds of glorious colors chatted in a gold cage that filled the center of the

167

living room. A fuzzy gray ball of a cat lounged on a white sofa.

"No, no! Not on the furniture!" Mrs. Davis shooed the cat out of the room. "Penny, you may leave your shoes there by the door while I clean up this mess. I don't know why advertisers keep sending me cats."

A puppy bounded down the hallway and threw itself at John. "Do you like dogs better?" he asked.

"What? Oh." Mrs. Davis came around the corner with a spray bottle in her hand. "I like all animals, just not in my new house. He has his own place outside. Out! Go on you!"

"Doesn't he have a name?" John watched the puppy slink away after the cats.

"We haven't had time to pick names yet." Mrs. Davis checked her hair in the hall mirror. "Maybe you can help us. Come wash your hands and I'll show you the rabbits."

She led the way through a library and a dining room before they finally ended up in the kitchen. Everything matched and everything gleamed.

"Did you have to polish this?" Penny caught her reflection in the kitchen table. "It must take you forever."

"We had to find a cleaning service." Mrs. Davis handed her a towel. "Trey has to travel for his stores and I have to travel for my show. Neither of us has the time to do much housework. We're lucky just to have a month home together." She sighed as her phone chirped. "I'd better take this call. But once you've washed up, you can peek at the animals outside." The phone chirped again and she carried it into an office.

Peering out the window, John wiped his hands on his t-shirt. "I see the bunnies."

"Two cats, five puppies and three rabbits." Penny stood over his shoulder to count. "Is that an iguana?"

"There's a snake in that cage. It's huge!"

"It's a boa constrictor." Mr. Davis carried groceries in from the garage. "You must be John – and of course I met the valiant defender the other day. Hello, Penny, and how do you do? I haven't gotten close to that snake, but I hear it's four feet long and growing. You can imagine Daphne's reaction when her producer dropped it off."

"I thought my producer was joking." Mrs. Davis returned and gave her husband a kiss. "I asked him if he was going to come feed the snake rats every night. Do you know what dead rats feel like?" She shuddered. "I liked it better when they had me read the weather on the news."

"Ha! Ha! Ha!" This time, when Mr. Davis laughed, it sounded real. "I doubt you miss reporting on hurricanes – or wading through snow banks. Isn't your job better now that you can swim with dolphins in Hawaii? Or see John here get rescued by a seal? Ha! I want to hear that story for myself."

"You'll have to wait," Mrs. Davis told him. "Penny and John need to start their homework before the other guests arrive. Why don't you two follow me? We set up the perfect spot for you."

Mrs. Davis showed them the comfortable chairs she'd pulled up to desks in a small den. "The computer is there if you need it," she said. "And in a little bit, I will bring you strawberries and cheese for a snack. If you can concentrate now and do well tomorrow, Abigail may let you visit again."

"I think she won't mind," Penny said, catching sight of a trampoline in the backyard.

"But we can't come every day," John said. "Sometimes we have to help Mr. Cavendish. And Abigail wants us to teach her how to cook spaghetti tomorrow."

"Today, at least, you do not have to worry about helping anyone." Mrs. Davis turned on a light by John's chair. "We plan to take care of everything."

Two Conversations

Over strawberries and brown bread toast, Mr. Davis quizzed Penny on her vocabulary list. He proofread John's math worksheet. Just as he was going to show them the spare toys he stored in the bathhouse, the doorbell rang.

"You know the kids who are coming," Mr. Davis told them as they left the den. "Some of them are your favorite people, Penny. Ha! We have Caitlin Keller and her mother from next door. Herbert, Tony, and Watt Parker all live down the street."

"Bert couldn't come," Watt was telling Mrs. Davis on the front step. "He had to work at Mal's Market after school. And Tony has baseball game. Dad said it would be ok if Hank came instead. He's my best friend."

"I hope you don't mind," Mrs. Parker apologized. "The boys said they knew John from school. I thought they could entertain one another."

"Hank wants to see your trampoline." Watt tugged Mrs. Davis' sleeve. "He doesn't believe you use it for exercise."

"It's out in the back yard." Mrs. Davis held the door wide so the boys could run through. She tried not

170

to look at the mud their sneakers left behind on her white carpet.

"This is my mother," Caitlin announced unnecessarily. She and her mother wore matching pink outfits.

"What a charming home," Mrs. Keller said, kissing the air by Mrs. Davis' cheek. "Of course it would be beautiful. You're so lovely yourself. And Trey, you are as handsome as Caitlin said. It's so wonderful to have you here. We hoped you would tear down the derelict on Postman's Hack, but this is much more comfortable."

"Ha! Ha! Ha!" Mr. Davis put his hands on Penny's shoulders. "We wouldn't touch that house. Such atmosphere there on the cliff – what a view it must have!"

"Penny and John are staying there now with the friendly woman who lives," Mrs. Davis said. "That old house is starting to turn into a real home, isn't it, Penny?"

Mrs. Keller pinched Mrs. Davis' cheek. "Isn't it like you to include them in your little party! I've never met foster children before."

Caitlin's eyes followed her mother's and narrowed. "Isn't that what you wore to school, Henny-Penny?"

"Why don't I show you kids the way to the pool?" Mr. Davis asked before Penny could answer back. "If you like, you can have a few trips down the waterslide while I get the grill started."

"We didn't bring bathing suits," Penny told him as they followed him outside.

"I did. I'm wearing my new bikini." Caitlin tossed her clothes on a deck chair and ran to the water slide. "Too bad, Henny-Penny! You don't get a turn!"

"If you were to check the bathhouse there," Mr. Davis nodded at a shed by a putting green, "I believe Daphne left something out. She tends to be prepared for contingencies."

"John!" Hank tripped over a deck chair, but that didn't stop him. "You've got to come help us. Watt found a laser tag game right under the trampoline and we want you to shoot at us."

"Go ahead, John," Mr. Davis said. "You might get a closer look at the rabbits. They like hiding under the trampoline."

"This is the best house ever." Hank clambered over the pool gate. "Did you see the boa constrictor, John? Watt said they let it out at night and it gets all the way over to his backyard. It almost ate him yesterday!"

"Come on." Watt was jumping out his impatience on the trampoline. "Hank, you and I jump first. We're out if John shoots one of our vests."

Hank hoisted himself up. "Wait until we tell Katie about coming here tomorrow at school. She'll be so jealous."

"I'll bet you're not used to a house like this," Watt told John. "I'll bet you've got nothing normal –"

John aimed and Watt's vest buzzed.

"You're hit!" Hank shouted. "I didn't even start jumping yet! You have to get off, Watt. I'm the winner!"

"I don't care." Watt tossed his vest to John. "This trampoline is ok, but it's not like the stuff you have on Postman's Hack – that flying carpet and broom and things. Note to mention that dragon in your basement."

"There's no dragon."

"A dragon? No way! You never told me about that, Watt." Hank flopped down, his own vest buzzing. "Hey! You can't hit me now. I didn't say to start."

"Too bad. It's my turn again."

John bounced as they argued. He jumped over every laser Hank shot, but Watt got him out on the next turn. It didn't matter. He had turns shooting and turns jumping. Without even noticing, John was almost having a good time.

Penny was, too. The new bathing suit fit her better than anything she'd ever owned and the waterslide was the best she'd ever seen. Even Caitlin stopped whispering insults at her. Mr. Davis laughed whenever Caitlin spoke to him, but when Penny asked him about the toys in the bathhouse, he took her seriously.

"I like figuring out what people will enjoy." Mr. Davis considered Penny. "For example, I thought you'd like the pool better than the toys in the bathhouse. Your brother will probably wander over to the animals before dinner."

"What about me?" Caitlin asked.

"We're storing some of Daphne's Halloween costumes in the bathhouse. I seem to recall something pink with a crown –" Caitlin scrambled out of the pool. "Ha! I thought that would send her running."

"You're good." Penny wrapped herself in a towel so she could help him at the grill. "No wonder you're so rich. Now you can buy things that are fun for you."

"It would be great if that were true." Mr. Davis laid out his tools for the grill. "In recent years, Daphne and I have wanted more things that can't be bought. From what I hear, it sounds as if you and your brother would understand. You can't buy a family." He flipped a spatula over in the air and caught it. "Ha! But what you

173

can't buy, you can sometimes invite over for dinner. How about I show you how to throw pizza dough?"

The doorbell rang again. More grown-ups arrived. Watt and Hank left the trampoline for the toys in the bathhouse. John lingered in the back yard to play with the puppies. In his head, he named them all: Roly, Poly, Moley, Foley, and Squint the Second.

"There you are, John," Mrs. Davis said, coming through a patio door. "Do you mind lending me a hand? Trey has Penny finishing the dough, but I need some help choosing pizza toppings. We don't have meat for you, but there's plenty of vegetables."

"That's ok." John followed her into the kitchen. On the wall, he noticed pictures of her from different episodes of her show. "Did you really ride an elephant?"

"Just for a short time. It was very dusty." As they washed their hands in the kitchen, Mrs. Davis described feeding lions and sharks on tv. While they shredded cheese, she told him about cuddling koala bears. Eventually, she steered the conversation towards him. "Mr. Cavendish said your mother died. I'm so sorry."

John dropped the cheese into a bowl. He didn't have anything to say about his mother.

"We had a baby who died." Mrs. Davis carried some peppers to the sink to wash. "We can't have any more children, but he would have been about your age." She swallowed. "Every day, we miss him. Just as your mother must miss you." She straightened up and turned off the faucet. "But I'm fortunate to have Trey. I'm glad you have your sister."

John still didn't say anything. He still missed his mother.

174

"There's my phone ringing again." Mrs. Davis wiped her hands. "You'll have to excuse me, John. My producers are trying to talk me into a helicopter flight for next week. While I argue with them, please decide what you think about cupcakes for dessert."

John thought cupcakes sounded like a good idea. In fact, John thought that the whole party had been a good idea. When Penny and John found Abigail at home, they talked over one another to tell her about it.

"Mrs. Davis only got her tv show because she's so good with animals. Once she had to do the news with a chimp and she got it talking and everything."

"Mr. Davis has his own airplane. He flies all over the country to visit his toy shops."

"They have five puppies. Mrs. Davis let me name them."

"He wants us to come back and try out their hot tub."

"They didn't ask the other kids."

"He's going to teach us how to golf."

"And how to sail."

"That will be wonderful," Abigail said. "I am so glad that you had a nice time. And dinner – did you eat enough? I made doughnuts." She pointed to a plate of charred gray balls on the counter. Even Squint didn't look interested.

"We ate too much pizza already," John said. "Mr. Davis can sling pizza dough around the room and catch it with one hand."

"They grilled it in an outdoor oven, just like it would be at a restaurant." Penny caught sight of Abigail's face and stopped. "You aren't sorry, are you? You're not mad we weren't here?"

"No, of course not." Abigail carried the doughnuts to the back porch and tossed them out for the birds. "I hoped you would have fun tonight."

Penny watched her back. "You knew we'd like it over there, didn't you? You knew they'd have all that stuff."

"They don't have everything," John cut in. "Mrs. Davis told me. She said that she can't have children and that's what she wants more than anything else."

"Then I am glad that you have become friends." Abigail stared at the sink, full of dishes, then dropped the doughnut plate in the garbage. She looked at the other dirty dishes, and then threw them away, too.

"Abigail —"

"Penelope Rose, I am afraid I am not up for talking much tonight." Abigail closed the lid on the trashcan. "I am just very glad it is time for bed."

"I'm too excited to go to bed," John declared. "I don't think I can fall asleep."

"Me neither," Penny said. She had too much to think over.

Squint made a comment from his chair, but Abigail pushed him onto the floor.

"It does not matter if you are ready or not," Abigail said. "It is time. Come along, John Tomas. Let us find that toothbrush of yours."

Two Voices in the Dark

After they'd climbed into bed, Penny stared into the darkness. Moonlight swirled over the little golden bottle John had picked out for her. Even across the room, the colors seemed to wave sympathetically.

176

"John?" Penny asked. "Did you notice tonight? Mr. and Mrs. Davis have a giant tv."

"I know." John yawned. "They have a pool and a trampoline. They've got everything."

"Yeah." Penny bunched up her pillow. "It's like what Abigail promised."

"Like what?"

"Like the family we bargained for. Abigail promised the pool and the pets – and there they are. Mr. and Mrs. Davis have more than we even wanted."

"No." John woke up a little more. He pushed himself onto his elbows. "It's not like that."

"They even have horses. Mrs. Davis said she keeps them in Texas for her father to ride."

John turned on the light. "What?"

"I just thought you should know. It's the family. Abigail is keeping her side of the bargain. She found them."

John sat up. "No, she didn't. We're not done helping yet. We haven't found all the stones."

Penny shifted onto her other side. "That wasn't part of the deal. Abigail is stronger now. She's doing things normally, just the way she wanted. We helped her figure out how to save her powers. And now she found us the perfect family."

"They're not perfect," John said. "They're vegetarians."

Penny rolled over. That didn't matter.

"And besides." John lay back down. "They don't want to adopt us. They didn't say anything about it."

"Not yet." Penny flipped onto her stomach. "But they will. You'll see."

John sat up. He lay back down again. He remembered washing dishes and walking home from school and picking strawberries with Abigail. He remembered the night they jumped on his bed and the night they found out about Seleumbra. The eclipse was just three weeks away.

"I don't want to leave," John said.

Penny reached over and turned off the light. She remembered the morning they had found their room transformed. She remembered scrubbing the bathtub and going for ice cream and watching the rugs fly down the hallway. She remembered the morning after they found out about Seleumbra. Their time was almost up. "There's nothing we can do about it now," she said.

Outside, the lighthouse called out a warning. A fog was rolling in.

Two Twists

They saw a lot of Mr. and Mrs. Davis over the next few weeks. Mr. Davis took them to his new store and had them test out video games. Mrs. Davis treated Penny to a haircut and then bought John new shoes. Squint came with them on Mr. Cavendish's boat over the weekends, but sometimes, they saw Abigail only at breakfast and bedtime. "Go enjoy yourselves," she said every time they left. "You ought to make new friends."

Penny and John needed to have other people around. When they were alone, ever since the night of the Davis' party, Penny and John couldn't stop arguing. John woke up cranky. He felt crankier at school. He forgot to be cranky with Mrs. Davis or Mr. Cavendish, but alone with Penny, he remembered. It didn't help that Penny got bossier each morning.

"Why can't you move faster?" Penny asked the Saturday before school ended. "Mr. Cavendish is going to be waiting."

"He's not." John stirred his cereal around in his bowl. "He'd send Bill up to get us if we were late."

Just then, Bill flew down over the window.

"See?" Penny said.

179

"We shouldn't go. It's raining again." John pushed his bowl away. "It's always raining now. It's rained for the past two weeks."

"It didn't rain yesterday."

"It drizzled."

"But it didn't rain."

Bill squawked at a crack of thunder.

John poured more cereal in his bowl. "We shouldn't go."

"You will be fine," Abigail said, holding out raincoats. "Mr. Cavendish will look after you. Hurry now."

A wet fog nearly blanketed Mr. Cavendish on the beach. Across the ocean, a dank wind blew, ominously cold and damp. The waves slammed against the rocks and the dinghy floundered against its anchor. Mr. Cavendish looked grim.

"Got to move quickly," he said. "One storm's passed through, but another's coming up fast."

"We would have been here on time, but John had to eat two bowls of cereal," Penny said, powering up the motor on the dinghy.

"I had to show Abigail how to change a light bulb. And you had toast."

"Sit up there, Penny, and hold tight, both of you," Mr. Cavendish said. "I'll steer today."

Penny and John sat on opposite sides of the dinghy, but as they moved into deeper water, they kept slipping onto buckets of bait. One wave nearly tipped Squint off the port side. Another nearly flung Mr. Cavendish off the stern. It was worse onboard the *Caddy*. The boat rocked so badly that John had to cling to the deck when he cleared the mooring. Penny stumbled when the boat rolled with a swell.

"Shouldn't we go back in?" John shouted over the wind.

"Scaredy cat," Penny shouted back. But she asked Mr. Cavendish, "Should we?"

"Got to go," Mr. Cavendish said, his voice gruffer in the wind. "Lobsters don't pay attention to the weather and neither do customers. But get your jackets on. Here's the rain again."

The rain flew up into their eyes, up their noses, down their jackets. Penny slid around the deck, getting gear ready. John sloshed through puddles of bait. "Hey," he said when Penny dropped a crate on his foot.

"Ouch," Penny said when John lost hold of a bucket. The boat dipped and she landed right on top of him.

"Get off me." John pushed her.

"Lay off." She pushed back.

"Head's up." Mr. Cavendish slowed the engine. "Here's the first pot."

He gave Penny the job of holding the boat in place as best she could against the waves. "If you have to steer, go into the valley and ride it out," he said. "John, you keep holding tight. You're in charge of taking the lobsters out of the trap."

Penny and John did the best they could, but it wasn't easy. The boat kept rolling and they both kept losing their footing. Several times, John dropped a lobster that scuttled away. Several times, Mr. Cavendish had to fight the wind to pull the lobster pots out of the water.

Then suddenly, the boat slapped down hard on the water. One of the lobster pots swung from its line.

181

Smack! The crate whacked Mr. Cavendish off his feet. With a grunt, he fell to the deck.

"Mr. Cavendish!" Penny screamed.

"He's knocked out!" John ran over. "His head is bleeding."

Bill and Burt darted down. Penny wanted to help, but when she let go of the wheel, a wave nearly swept the boat upside down. Squint and Caddy screeched at her to pay attention. "John, you've got to call the Coast Guard. I can't hold the boat steady at the same time."

John tried to press the right buttons down as the boat leaped and dropped. He tried to give the Coast Guard clear information. "I think they said to stay put," he told Penny. "They said they'll come."

But the ocean didn't let them wait. It tossed the *Caddy* from the crest of one wave to the top of another. Water swept over the sides and swished on the deck. The last lobster pot swung from the hauler, dragging the boat hard to port, then harder to starboard. Squint clung to a pile of wet ropes and yowled again.

"I know," Penny yelled back to him. "But I can't steer. That lobster pot – it's pulling us over."

Bill and Burt swooped up to help cut the line, but the wind tossed them away. John wiped rain from his eyes. "I can do it."

John found the knife Mr. Cavendish wore on his belt and stumbled over to the hauler. Behind him, he felt Penny tie a rope to his lifejacket, but he didn't look back. With first one foot up on the rail, then the other foot, John teetered with his hands gripping the top of the cabin. Every time the boat rocked, he had to duck to avoid the lobster pot. John reached up and made one cut – then another – John made a final cut and with a wide swing, the pot fell into the water. "It's off," he called.

Penny didn't answer. The ocean was dragging the boat through a channel between two islands. It was the wrong way home, she knew, and parts of the channel were dangerous and shallow. Caddy screamed, but no matter how hard Penny pulled the wheel, she couldn't get the boat to turn. Caddy screamed again.

"It won't move!" Penny leaned all her weight to starboard, but the *Caddy* streamed forward.

"Penny!" John pointed off the bow. Ahead of them, channels of water churned and swirled down to the ocean floor. "Penny! We've got to move! It's a whirlpool."

Penny threw herself at the wheel. Caddy screeched over her head. Clinging to the top of the cabin, John watched the whirlpool come closer and closer. Suddenly, the bow bobbed high into the air. Rain twisted in the sky. The motor sputtered. Penny caught her balance and heaved the wheel to starboard again.

They were free.

The wind swept over them out to open ocean, and with it went the strongest waves. The clouds lifted, leaving behind a shower of rain. Laughing, Caddy swung high into the air. Bill and Burt flew after her. Squint spat at the floor and began a lecture.

Penny didn't listen. "John? Are you ok? How's Mr. Cavendish?"

"He's all pale and bloody, but he's breathing." John dropped down to her at the wheel. "Hey, Penny? Look at what I found. It just flew out of the whirlpool. I caught it."

In the palm of his hand, in a little green bottle, lay three red stones.

"'Three there in the air where you swirl all direction.'" Penny stared at John. "That's what it said on the painting in the living room."

John nodded. "It was another clue."

Two New Perspectives

"Mr. Cavendish said that we needed to learn how to use the radio weeks ago," Penny said that night as they sat around the kitchen table. "He said it was the most important lesson he could teach us — that, and to keep our life jackets on."

"He taught you how to steer," John said. "You were good at getting us through that whirlpool."

"And you were fabulous at cutting that lobster trap off." Penny took a sip of purple tonic. "Abigail, you'd have been amazed. John kept his balance the whole time. And the boat was heaving all over the place."

"Mrrow," said Squint from his own bowl of tonic on the floor.

"I am so proud of you," Abigail said. "Mr. Cavendish was very lucky that you were with him. The doctors say that he will be out of the hospital soon, but if you had not been there, he might not have come home at all."

"And John found you another bottle."

Abigail kissed him on the head. "I am proud of that, too."

Mrs. Davis shook her head at her husband. From their kitchen, she'd seen the Coast Guard carry Mr. Cavendish ashore. When Penny and John had appeared, she'd called Mr. Davis to help them home. Both Mr. and Mrs. Davis looked more shaken and frightened than Penny, John or Abigail had been that entire afternoon.

"I still can't believe you made it home," Mrs. Davis said. "Lobstering is dangerous work, even in nice weather. On a day like today, you should have been safe at home."

"Or visiting us," Mr. Davis said. "I have a new order of video games that you can try."

"We had to help Mr. Cavendish," Penny said. "We have to pay him back somehow. He spent all of Thursday getting the lights to work in the hallway."

"And last week he stopped the sink from coughing up turnip tops," John said. "We owe him a lot."

"Ha!" Mr. Davis didn't understand. "Next time, why don't you let Abigail take care of Mr. Cavendish? She's the adult, after all."

Abigail's face burned. "That is what my books would say."

"We're all taking care of each other," John told her. "We help Mr. Cavendish and he helps you and you clean the bathrooms."

"And you taught me to wash the dishes."

John grinned at her. "And sometimes you can cook."

"These cookies actually came out well." Penny popped one last bite into her mouth. "There's hardly any cookie with all the raisins and chocolate, but they taste pretty good. Once school ends, maybe I can teach you how to bake a cake."

Mrs. Davis' phone chirped, but she ignored it. "I'm concerned that you are teaching and cleaning and working too much. You should be playing like children, not acting like heroes."

John sat up. "We're heroes?"

"I am," Penny said. "You're too short."

"You're too fat."

"You're too dumb."

John kicked her under the table and Penny laughed, nearly choking on her tonic.

Mrs. Davis excused herself to answer her phone. As she talked, Penny watched her take note of the chicken bones Squint had forgotten under a cabinet. When he shook their hands good night, Mr. Davis made a face as he smelled old fish in their clothes. With a hint of worry in their voices, they said good-bye. Penny sighed.

"Mrs. Davis is right," Abigail said. "You were heroes today. You should receive a reward."

"It's ok." Penny yawned.

John nodded. "It's been fun. Today wasn't so much fun, but it was exciting."

Squint, dozing into his milk, let out a sleepy, "Mrrow."

"You said it best, Captain Zach," Abigail said. "Take that last sip, Penelope Rose, and we will get you ready for bed."

"You didn't call him Squint," John said as they climbed the stairs.

"No, he acted like a real sea captain today." Abigail steered John toward the bathroom. "Did I ever tell you what happened when Captain Zach tried fishing?"

As they brushed their teeth, Abigail explained that once One-Eyed Zach had caught a tiny oyster in his nets. "That oyster was the only thing he caught that day, and the poor thing had a speck of sand caught in its mouth. Captain Zach pried the sand out, tossed it overboard and then sent the oyster on its way. But as the speck sank, it turned the water clear, straight down

186

to the sea floor. One-Eyed Zach had not realized the sand had been a miniscule, magical pearl. It had not been an ordinary oyster."

Abigail picked up John's clothes from the floor and hung them on a lamp. "After that, sailors called the spot Zach's Folly. That pearl could have turned him into a powerful illusionist. And he threw it away without thinking."

Penny took John's clothes off the lamp and carried them to a laundry basket. "It sounds like One-Eyed Zach never did anything right," she said. "He was always making mistakes."

"Poor Captain Zach," John said.

Abigail leaned on the windowsill where she could see the moon. "You know, Zach's Folly is one of the most beautiful things on Seleumbra," she said. "It is like a window into the sea. Some sailors spend hours watching schools of fish swim through it."

"So his mistake wasn't a bad after all."

"That's what Magic would say." Penny folded the covers back on John's bed. "She says something good can come out of every mistake."

"Magic is right." Abigail looked up at the sky. "Even from being banished, I believe some good will come of it."

John came to the window. The moon showed the large shadow of Seleumbra. "Do you really miss being at home?"

"Every day." Abigail lifted the window open. With the storm past, they could smell lilies and grass and briny ocean. Leaning over the windowsill, she breathed deeply. "I miss my garden and the fairies that came to visit. I miss knowing how to do things properly. But," she drew John closer, "I will miss things here, too. Look out there."

"What?"

"Just look," Abigail answered. The crescent of moon shimmered on the ocean. The pine trees whispered to the waves. The waves hushed them to sleep. Clouds parted and they could see a speckling of stars. John leaned onto her arm and yawned.

Suddenly, Abigail fell. Penny leaped forward and John leaped up. Frantically, they grabbed at her hands, but they couldn't pull her back in time. Abigail pulled them out, out and over the garden, over the pine trees and over the ocean. On a puff of gentle air, they were flying.

Penny screamed. John shouted. Abigail only laughed and squeezed their hands tightly. A puff of air carried them around the lighthouse, up and over the fort in the bay. John gasped and pointed at seals sleeping on rocks. Penny exclaimed and pointed out two humpback whales flipping their tales. And just as they grew a little tired, Abigail sat them down high in the sky. A soft, cool cloud wrapped around them.

"That's Hope Island." John pointed at the dark shadow on the water. "Look, you can see something twinkling."

"Fairy lights," Abigail said. "They are gathering, I think. There is a new moon coming."

"And there's the baseball field." John looked in the other direction. "It's all lit up. They're having a game."

"Abigail," Penny said. "You didn't have to take us flying. You're supposed to be saving your strength."

"I have been saving my strength," Abigail said. "I do not even feel ill now, although I certainly must be using a lot of my powers. I can afford a treat for you, especially after all you have done."

John sat up. "We're not done yet," he said. "You don't have all the stones. And we didn't get you any sea lettuce. We forgot."

"There is plenty on shore." Abigail shook herself. "And it does not matter. Squint and I will have to do the best we can. It is time."

"You can't go." John crossed his arms. "We haven't been adopted."

"Not yet."

"No," Abigail agreed. "No, not yet."

"Maybe you'll have to stay – just to keep the bargain. You'll have to stay until we've got the perfect family."

"I remember." Abigail squeezed John's foot. "Not to worry. And look – the baseball game must be over."

With a blast, bursts of fireworks shot towards the stars. Below, in the baseball stadium, the fans cheered. Up in the cloud, John reached over and gave Abigail a fierce hug.

"You are most welcome," Abigail said. Her voice sounded thicker than usual.

On her other side, Penny watched them. John didn't let Abigail go for a long time.

189

Three Departures

The next morning, they woke up to a loud banging.

"Tell Abigail the house will collapse if she hammers like that," Penny mumbled into her pillow. "The walls can't take it."

"I don't think it's Abigail." John looked out the window. "Someone's at the door."

"You go." Penny rolled over. "I'm staying in bed all morning."

Half asleep, John shuffled into the hallway. Six little bells rang the hour in the living room, but the person on the porch kept pounding. Rubbing sleep out of his eyes, John opened the door.

Mrs. Collins shoved him aside with her bag. "It's about time," she said. "I thought I had to be here early before you set out lobstering. Where's Miss McKinney? We need to talk."

John shrugged.

"Your sister's around, I suppose?" Mrs. Collins strode down the hall to the kitchen. "Or is she off rescuing someone else?" Mrs. Collins stopped at a basket of seaweed sitting on the table. "Miss McKinney!" she bellowed. "I want to talk to you."

Penny stumbled down the back stairs into the kitchen. "What are you doing here?" she asked.

Mrs. Collins grunted. "You've grown out of your clothes, the both of you. I heard that you've spent the past few weeks being part-time lobstermen. Housecleaners, too. I thought we already talked about labor laws. Miss McKinney!"

Out of the window, John saw Abigail lugging a basket through the garden. Through the screen in the door, Penny saw Squint spring onto the steps.

"Hrrow," Squint said.

"Good morning, Mrs. Collins," Abigail called as she climbed up the steps. "This is a surprise for an early hour of the morning." Balancing the basket on her hip, she maneuvered through the back door. "Did you come for breakfast? We did not expect company."

"From what I hear, I should have come sooner." Mrs. Collins wrinkled her nose. "What are you carrying? Dead crabs?"

Abigail dropped the basket on the floor. "Sea lettuce," she said. "I am collecting things for a project. A concoction, John Tomas calls it."

"It's an ocean project," Penny stopped her. "An experiment. It's science."

"Really." Mrs. Collins narrowed her eyes. "You're doing a science experiment two days before school ends?"

"We love learning," Penny told her.

"I'll say." Mrs. Collins pulled out a chair and sat down with her legs wide apart. "It was quite a phone call I received last night. Trey Davis says I have been derelict in my duty – neglecting the children and permitting them to get into trouble. Is that true, Miss McKinney?"

Abigail sank into a chair. "I do not understand."

191

Mrs. Collins snorted. "Of course not. You never wanted me to check into how you were raising the children. Fortunately, it doesn't matter now. Mr. and Mrs. Davis are prepared to take them. Somehow, Missy, here, and her little brother have made a good impression. Mr. Davis even spoke of adoption, but we'll see how that goes."

"No," John said. He nudged Penny to do something.

Penny didn't know what to do. "Abigail didn't do anything wrong," she said.

"I warned you. I said I said I'd move you if you did anything odd." Mrs. Collins took a file from her bag. "And move you I will. You're lucky to have this opportunity. Mr. and Mrs. Davis have such reputations that we can rush most of the paperwork. We're going to transfer you right away."

"No," John said. "We're staying here."

"You're going to get packing, Buster. They are expecting you for breakfast." Mrs. Collins laid the papers out on the table. "I'll give you five minutes. You'll need to sign these, Miss McKinney."

"Five minutes?" Penny was stunned.

John crossed his arms. "No."

Abigail looked stricken. "We never expected anything to change so quickly. Surely, you would not mind if the children left later. I could leave them this evening. It would give us time for a farewell party."

Mrs. Collins waved a pen at her. "We can't ask the Davis family to wait. They're important people. And I have a schedule, too, you know."

"We're not going." John planted his feet. "You can't make us."

192

Mrs. Collins grunted. "I can and I will, Buster. Go pack your things."

Abigail took a step forward. "Perhaps if I could talk to the children alone—"

"They'll be fine." Mrs. Collins held out a pen.

"But if you gave us a moment —"

"Miss McKinney," Mrs. Collins stood up, "I'm usually very patient, but not today, not after the night I had. Missy, here can take care of her brother. They're not your concern any more." She jabbed a finger at Penny. "Up you go, you two. I'll give you three minutes. And don't look at me like I'm torturing you. I thought you wanted to be adopted."

"No." John jerked himself away and pounded up the stairs. He threw their bedroom door open and fell down hard against the wall. His ears rang, but he heard Penny close the door behind him. John clenched his fists. "I don't want to go," he told her. "I like it here. It's funny."

"It's messed up." Penny slumped down next to him. She noticed the dust underneath their beds. A beetle darted into the closet. "You remember the sandwiches Abigail made? Or the way the sink used to burp?" Penny nudged him, but John didn't even pretend to smile. Penny sighed. "Abigail misses her cottage, John. She said so last night. And Captain Zach must hate being a cat. They have to go."

John pulled his knees to his chest. "It's not fair."

Penny nudged him again. "We did alright back when Mom was sick. And at the hospital and at the shelter afterwards. Yesterday, we got the boat to the mooring without Mr. Cavendish or anybody."

John clenched his fists. That wasn't why he was mad.

Penny stared at her feet. "Maybe you liked it here," she said. "Maybe I did, too. That's not important now. It wasn't the deal. Abigail promised to find us the perfect family and now we've got them. We promised to help her and now she's leaving. That was the bargain."

John kicked his foot on the floor. "Everyone's always leaving."

Penny touched his leg. "I'm not."

"Yes, you are too leaving." Mrs. Collins barged through the door. "Get off the floor and into your shoes, Buster. You're late already."

Mrs. Collins didn't turn her back as they changed into jeans and she didn't let them go into the kitchen to say good-bye. Abigail and Squint came down the hallway, but Mrs. Collins shoved Penny and John out the door. "We won't say anything," Mrs. Collins said over her shoulder. "It's messy and takes too much time."

Squint hissed.

Abigail called from the doorway, "John Tomas, Penelope Rose, dear, thank you – thank you for everything."

Mrs. Collins snorted and pushed John into her car. Penny wrenched her arm free. "Abigail?" she asked. "You're sure you'll be ready? You'll be ok?"

Abigail's eyes sparkled, but she straightened her shoulders. "We will manage."

"Come on." Mrs. Collins yanked Penny's arm. "Someone might think that you weren't grateful."

Three Surprises

John wasn't grateful. It didn't matter that Mr. and Mrs. Davis had piled the table high with freshly squeezed orange juice, cocoa with whipped cream, chocolate chip pancakes and waffles with strawberries. John sulked through it all. He stared at the ceiling when Mr. Davis found him a model robot for his new bedroom. He ignored Roly and Poly when they snuck inside begging to play. He refused to budge when Mrs. Davis suggested they shop for new clothes.

"It's not you," Penny told Mrs. Davis when John stalked away to a corner. "It's just that it happened so fast."

"We'll give it time, then," Mrs. Davis said. "No, don't clear the dishes, Penny. The cleaners will take care of them. How about you come along with my film crew today? They're making me helicopter out to film humpback whales."

Still, riding a helicopter through clouds was not the same as sitting on a cloud itself. John didn't bother looking out the window. Mrs. Davis talked about polar bears with her crew, even mentioning that Penny and John could go with her to see ice burgs that summer. John still didn't care.

"I want to go home," John said to Penny when she went to his room to say goodnight.

Penny set the photographs of their mother beside his bed. She should have found a way to get a picture of Abigail and Squint. "It's too late."

"John?" Mrs. Davis knocked gently on the door.

Mr. Davis opened it wide. "We would like to suggest an outing to Postman's Hack tomorrow. It would give you a chance to talk things over with Abigail."

"We can go after school," Mrs. Davis said. "Trey has a new bicycle for each of you, so we can ride to your old house when you're finished. Because it's the last day, we'll have plenty of time for a visit."

"Ha! Now you have something to look forward to," Mr. Davis said. "See if you can get to sleep now, John."

The next day, everyone in John's class was excited about the last day of school – everyone but John. All he could think about was what he wanted to say to Abigail.

"Is it true?" Hank prodded him in the back while they cleared out their desks. "Are you living in the toy house now? What happened with the witch?"

"We saw you the other night." Watt jabbed John from the other side. "We saw you flying. You flew up over the trees and everything."

"It was amazing." Hank bounced up and down in his chair. "I'd give anything to fly like that."

John stared down at the bottom of his desk. There was a squashed paper dodecahedron jammed in the corner. He hadn't realized before, but it looked like the golden stopper.

"Are you really getting adopted?" Hank asked. "I heard Mrs. Sok on the phone this morning. The witch got into trouble for making you go on that lobster boat. Now you get to live with Daphne Davis and the millionaire."

"I wouldn't want to," Watt leaned back in his chair. "I mean, sure, you'll probably meet all kinds of movie stars. They'll probably put you on tv on the *Daphne Davis* show or something. But if it were up to me, I'd stick with the witch."

John looked up from the dodecahedron. "Why?"

"With a witch, you never know what can happen," Watt said. "Any day, she might chop your ear off for lunch."

"She wouldn't, would she, Watt? You think?"

"No." John tried to flatten out the dodecahedron. Each piece had five identical sides.

"I can't believe John is still walking around with all his body parts." Watt folded his arms behind his head. "Nope, if I were in your place, I'd make them bring me back to Postman's Hack. I wouldn't leave for anything."

"Watt, if you're done cleaning, you can come help me wipe off the board." Mrs. Sok pulled out his chair. "You can talk to your friends after school lets out."

In Penny's class, Mr. Keenes spent the entire morning talking. First, Mr. Keenes had to talk where they would go for middle school. Then he had to talk about the books they had to read before starting middle school. He talked about his retirement and he talked about the graduation assembly that afternoon. "It's not everyone who deserves an award," he said. "But everyone who gets an award deserves your respect. So keep your feet off the chairs and your hands in your laps. I don't want to see eye-rolling from any new girls, either. Let's just get through this."

The fifth graders shuffled into the gym and sat before a large group of parents. Mr. and Mrs. Davis waved at her, but Penny didn't know why they bothered to come. Caitlin jumped up so often for awards that it looked like she didn't know how to sit still. Penny stopped listening after awhile. She was worried about John.

"And now, I would like to recognize a student who has not been with us very long," Mrs. LaFontaine said. "After a brief adjustment, this young lady demonstrated responsibility and academic promise in all subjects. She showed bravery two extraordinary emergencies at sea. It has been my pleasure to watch Penny Martinez develop the poise and quick thinking we hope all young ladies will have. Congratulations, Penny."

Tony had to poke Penny before she realized her name had been called. Making sure Mrs. Davis was watching, Mr. Keenes gave Penny a hug on her way to the podium. Mrs. LaFontaine handed Penny a certificate. During the applause, she said, "Although you are residing with Mr. and Mrs. Davis now, I thought Miss McKinney might want to be here, too. It's unfortunate that I couldn't reach her with an invitation."

"She works today," Penny said.

"No, I tried her at the Magic Shop. Apparently, she resigned yesterday." Mrs. LaFontaine guided Penny off the stage. "Enjoy your vacation, Penny. I'm quite proud of you."

Three Stops

Penny didn't have time to tell John about Abigail quitting her job at the Magic Shop. After school, he jumped on his new bicycle and rode as fast as he could to Postman's Hack Road. On their own bicycles, Mr. and Mrs. Davis meandered behind, trying to tell Penny how pleased they were.

"It's just a piece of paper," Penny said.

"It's not," Mrs. Davis said. "Mrs. LaFontaine didn't talk about anyone else the way she talked about you.

She wanted to make sure everyone heard how remarkable you are."

"I have a proposal," Mr. Davis said. "After you visit Abigail, let's head to Mal's Market. A bouquet of roses is more fun than a certificate."

But the clouds overhead weren't in the mood to celebrate. They hung heavy and low, dark and grim. When John arrived at the house, it looked grim, too. The pine trees bristled in the wind. And the door stayed reproachfully shut.

"She's not here," John said.

"Are you sure?" Mr. Davis climbed up the steps and twisted the doorknob. "It's not locked."

"Abigail never locks the door," Penny said. "Nobody ever wants to come in."

"Maybe she didn't hear us." Mrs. Davis knocked on the door. "Abigail? We've brought Penny and John to see you."

The door swung open. But nobody was there.

"Abigail!" John headed for the attic. "Abigail! We're back!"

"Go on ahead." Mr. Davis nudged Penny after him. "We'll wait in the living room. Tell Abigail about your prize."

Mr. and Mrs. Davis moved into the next room, but Penny stayed in the hallway. She heard the clock counting down the time. She heard the wind crying into the trees. She heard John's footsteps on the floor upstairs and then up in the attic. The house quivered. She knew why.

"Hello?" Mr. Cavendish called from the kitchen. "You back already?"

Penny found him at his toolbox. "You're supposed to be home in bed. What are you doing here?"

199

"Shutting things down." Mr. Cavendish ducked under the sink. "Can't have a gas leak."

John appeared from the back stairs. "Everything's gone," he said. "The cauldron and the recipe and everything."

"Mrs. LaFontaine said that Abigail quit work.." Penny turned away so she wouldn't have to see John's face.

"Yep." Mr. Cavendish kept working. "Gone this morning."

"But they can't have left." John folded his arms across his chest. "Abigail doesn't have all of Evie's stones, does she? And the stopper, we lost that awhile ago and it might be important." John rubbed his eyes with his fist. "She didn't even say good-bye."

"Didn't sound like she had a chance, the way you got hurried out." Mr. Cavendish stood up and wiped his hands, still with his back to them. "With you gone, she didn't have much reason to stick around."

"There's you," Penny said. "She could have stayed for you. You could have asked her."

Mr. Cavendish grunted. "Did that once before and it made no difference. Made it more painful for everyone, in fact. No, I learned my lesson. Better to let folks go. They're happier in their own place."

Outside the window, Bill flew down to the grass. Burt squawked up a warning.

"Ha! Ha! Ha! I thought I heard a voice back here." Mr. Davis crossed the kitchen to reach out a hand to Mr. Cavendish. "Good to see you out of the hospital. How is your head feeling?"

"Fine. Best be back to bed, though." Mr. Cavendish picked up his toolbox. "I'll come back later to deal with the bathrooms. You'd better take what's left from your bedroom. Nobody will need it anymore."

They watched him close the back door. "So Abigail's still at work, is she? Ha! I know you're disappointed, John, but we can come another time." Mr. Davis patted John's shoulder. "Let's go find Daphne. I left her on the phone in the living room"

They found Mrs. Davis examining the paintings on the wall. "Such interesting artwork," she said as she closed up her phone. "It's a pity they're so filthy. Did you notice the solar eclipse in the painting? It's like the eclipse we're having tonight."

"Now's the eclipse?" Penny asked. "It's timed for today?"

"Just after midnight. I might still have an article about it at home." Mrs. Davis squeezed John's hand. "I'm sorry Abigail isn't here. We can try tomorrow."

John shook his head. Abigail was going to leave with the eclipse. It would be the best time, she had said.

The clock whirred to strike the hour. The clock told the time. John spun around, wondering. And tonight, it was time for Abigail to go back.

"We can ride by again on our way back from Mal's Market," Mr. Davis said. "She may be home by then. It's four o'clock now."

"Hold on."

"She's not coming back, John," Penny said.

"No. Wait for the clock."

The two little men danced out of the two little doors. They whirled and twirled, but this time, they did not hold little circles. They did not hold crescents or semi-circles either. When they met, the little men held out tiny golden stones, each a miniature pentagon.

201

"Don't let them go back!" John rushed forward. But the little men did not dance back into the clock as usual. They waited for Mr. Davis to take the three stones from their hands. Then with a peal of bells, they whirled and twirled back behind their doors. The doors closed with a click.

"Penny," John said.

"'Time gives golden treasures when it is time.'" Penny looked from him to the painting and back again.

"That is just what it says on the wall." Mrs. Davis read the needlepoint again.

"What a wonderful clock." Mr. Davis examined it more closely. "Ha! Notice the numbers? It counts the phases of the moon, not just the time. That's why there are 28 numbers."

"And now, I suppose, must be the right time." Mrs. Davis zipped up her jacket. "At any rate, it is time for us to be going. We promised Penny some flowers."

"Penny." John still hadn't moved. "Penny, Abigail needs the stones."

"I know." But there was no way to get them to Abigail now.

Mr. Davis patted John's shoulder. "If you think Abigail needs these rocks, you'd better keep hold of them. Put them in your pocket. She'll count on you to give them back when you see her again."

But he wasn't going to see her again, John thought. She was gone. Abigail had left so quickly, she didn't even have everything for the rocket concoction. She'd fulfilled her side of the bargain and disappeared. She hadn't even said good-bye.

Suddenly, John was angry. He ran out of the living room and tugged open the front door. He didn't care that the ceiling collapsed behind him. He didn't care that the gate fell off when he grabbed his bicycle. Pedaling furiously, he jerked up the bicycle to jump over potholes. He dragged his feet to skid around corners. He passed kids from school and tourists' cars, but at Mal's Market, he threw his bicycle down. He grabbed a cart and shoved it through the doors that opened automatically. He shoved it again past a display of dish detergent. He was going to get Penny's flowers and then he was going to go to the Davis' mansion and forget all about Abigail and her ugly cat. John pushed his cart and hit a customer, but he didn't apologize. He pushed his cart again, and this time he hit a pyramid of grapefruit balanced on a table. The grapefruit cascaded to the floor. Then oranges toppled off their display. Then lemons began falling, followed immediately by the cantaloupes. And the peaches.

"What are you doing?" Mal demanded. She marched up to him and jabbed him in the leg. "What problem do you have with fruit?"

"Sorry," John said. But he wasn't sorry at all.

"Sorry is not going to cut it, young man." Mal took a bite of a cigar. "Where is that guardian of yours? I want to hear what she has to say."

"You can't." Breathless, Penny ducked around customers and fell onto John's shoulder. "Abigail's gone. That's why he's mad."

Mal spat into the glop on the floor. "What do you mean, she is gone?"

"We're living with Mr. and Mrs. Davis now. They're coming."

"I hope they are coming." Mal took another bite of cigar. "Just look at this mess."

Squashed peaches and melons dotted the floor. Customers kicked bruised limes out of the aisles. One of the clerks slipped on a smear of plum on the floor. He fell splat onto a watermelon. A pile of cabbages tumbled onto his head. "Ouch!" He held up his hands as the cabbage rained down.

"It looks like something Abigail would have done," Penny said to John. She couldn't help it. She began to smile.

Even John had to grin a little. "Maybe the sprinklers will go off."

Onions rained down on the clerk from the opposite bin. Then a bin of potatoes started to fall.

Mal stomped her foot. "Herbert Harris Parker," she bellowed, "pick yourself up and get the floor cleaned." She turned to John. "I will expect you to pay me back for this."

"Of course." Mr. Davis skidded up to them on a squashed bit of tomato. "We certainly will make this up to you."

"What happened, John?" Mrs. Davis helped her husband upright. "You shouldn't be laughing, Penny. I hope you've apologized. This is a terrible mess."

John rolled a lemon around with his foot. He still wasn't sorry, but he wasn't so mad anymore, either.

Mr. Davis reached for his wallet. "How much do we owe you, Mal?"

"You shouldn't pay for all this," Penny said. "It's John's fault. We should work it off or something."

"You're too young to be working," Mrs. Davis said. "And this has been a difficult day. We're all getting used to one another."

"I'll say." Mr. Davis smiled at her. "But not to worry. Ha! In a few weeks, I'll bet we'll be the perfect family."

"With the perfect children." Mrs. Davis patted John's shoulder.

But John rolled his eyes. Penny shuffled her feet. Mal chewed on her cigar and grunted.

Three People Worrying

Mr. and Mrs. Davis tried to understand why Penny and John wouldn't eat any dinner that night.

"The lasagna is all organic," Mrs. Davis said, "with eggplant and ricotta cheese and a special sauce from the farm stand. You have to try it."

"My father taught me how to make garlic bread," Mr. Davis added. "Ha! Ha! Ha! You've never had anything like it."

"Try the beet salad, John. It's very sweet, especially with the oranges."

"I'm sure you'll see Abigail soon." Mr. Davis poured them glasses of water. "She can't be gone forever."

John pushed his plate away. Without a word, he went to his room. Moley barked at him through the patio door, but he paid no attention. He had something he had to do.

Slowly, Penny followed him upstairs. Back at the table, she could hear Mr. and Mrs. Davis talking in concerned voices. They weren't happy. John wasn't happy. Somebody had to do something. Penny paused on the landing. Out the window, rain splattered onto the water in the swimming pool. Penny came to a decision.

She found John taking apart the robot in his bedroom.

"I've been thinking," Penny said, leaning against his doorway. "Abigail might not be able to leave, even if the eclipse is tonight. You said it. She doesn't have all the ingredients for her concoction."

John didn't answer. He pulled out a long twist of copper wire from the robot and laid it on the floor. Slowly, John bent the wire around the edge of one of the stones the clock had given them.

"Without those stones, Abigail might be stuck here." Penny kneeled on the floor next to him. "If she is, I bet we can live with her again. I bet Mr. and Mrs. Davis will understand. They'd probably be real nice about it. If you're really unhappy, they could make the Hairy Boar take us back."

John folded the wire, bending and wrapping it to make a design. As he worked, he checked to make sure each space would hold a stone precisely. Once he'd made 12 spaces, he bent the wire up. Gradually, the design began to look like a tiny soccer ball.

"John?" Penny frowned. "What are you doing?"

"It's the stopper." John twisted the last bit of copper wire so that the ball would hold together. "I made one at school that looked better, but I had to use paper. It wouldn't have worked for Abigail."

"I don't get it," Penny said. "I thought you didn't want Abigail to go."

"Mr. Cavendish said to let her."

"But you don't want to."

John shrugged.

"That's the point I was trying to make. Listen." Penny took his hand. "You want her to stay, don't you? All we have to do is wait here with the stones. I'll bet anything Abigail will mess up that concoction tonight without them. And then we'll have her back. It'll be like it was before."

"No, it won't." John put the stones in his pocket. "She needs us. It's like she said about Captain Zach. Even if we don't like it, we have to help. She's our responsibility."

"So what are you going to do? Go out searching?" Penny glanced out the window. "It's pouring rain. And you don't even know where she is."

"She's at the island." John pulled on his sneakers. "We've used everything in the living room to find the clues. Every picture except one."

"That sketch of Hope Island." Penny watched him tie his shoe laces. She watched him put the wire dodecahedron in his pencil box from school. But when John tried to put the box in his sweatshirt pocket, Penny rolled her eyes and put it in his backpack. "You're sure then? You really want to help Abigail?"

John reached for his jacket. "Yeah."

Penny slung the backpack over her shoulders. "Then we'll go out the window. Mr. and Mrs. Davis won't be happy about us leaving. We can take the *Caddy* to the island."

"You don't have to come."

Penny shoved open the window. "Don't be stupid." She crawled onto the roof and held a hand back for him. "And try to stay quiet. If you bang your feet, they'll hear."

Rain pounded against them as they climbed over a balcony. Rain gushed down the water slide and carried them down to the garden.

John peeked at Mr. and Mrs. Davis still sitting at the table. "They're talking."

"They're worried. Don't let them see you." Penny ducked around the trampoline and led the way to the beach. All of Mr. Cavendish's lights were off. The dinghy was in its usual place on the sand. They tried to be quiet, but as they dragged the dinghy down the beach, Caddy woke up with a squawk.

"Quiet," John told her, waving his arms so she'd stopping flapping in his face. "You're going to get us in trouble."

"Maybe she can get us to Hope Island," Penny said. "It's ok, Caddy. We're just going after Abigail."

With a cry, the seagull soared onto the wind to the lobster boat. Together, Penny and John dragged the dingy into the water and hoisted themselves over the sides. Penny started the motor and John peered through the rain. The sky, the water – everything was dark in the rain. Only Caddy, gleaming white, stood out against the fog.

"I can't see anything. Just Caddy up there."

"She'll tell us which way to go." Penny wiped rain out of her eyes. "Hold tight. I don't like the size of these waves."

The further they motored towards the lobster boat, the rougher the water became. Waves splashed up and over the sides of the dinghy. The current pulled the dinghy towards the rocks. "There's the boat," John pointed into a pool of clouds. "Slow down and I'll get on."

Caddy perched on the cabin above the steering wheel. Penny started the motor and John cast the boat off the mooring. As Penny steered out of the cove, Caddy soared ahead, crying out directions over the wind.

John hopped down beside Penny. "There are things out there on the water."

Penny looked over her shoulder. Through the rain and the fog, she couldn't see anything but night – except maybe a whiff of cloud reaching up, floating above the water. At least she thought it was a cloud.

"Listen," John said. "Don't you hear? They're talking."

It was true. Out in the water, voices were murmuring, rising up out of the water and speaking words Penny and John couldn't understand. Through the fog, they saw figures, ghostly figures, drifting beside them, all moving towards Hope Island.

John stepped closer to Penny. Sometimes a wrinkled hand reached up over the side of the boat. Sometimes a voice spoke right off the stern. Caddy squawked and flew into the wind, but even the wind had voices singing.

"It's sparkling," Penny whispered. "Look at the clouds. There are things sparkling in them."

Caddy screamed. John shouted. Penny pulled the wheel hard to port to avoid a rotten ship bursting up out of the water. Tall men, shiny with scales and glistening with seawater, shouted words in funny languages. With a splash, another ship leaped out of the water, then another and another.

Penny tugged the wheel in the opposite direction. "Hold on!"

The hull of the *Caddy* thumped against something. Penny pulled hard and the boat scraped along something else.

Something slimy and wet grasped John's hand before sliding back into the ocean. Something cold and shadowy slipped across his back before disappearing into the fog. He ducked below the cabin and watched as ghostly figures dragged themselves onto ships gaping with holes and shrunken wood. They heard corks popping and music playing, but every ship was sailing towards Hope Island.

"Almost there," Penny said. "Hang onto something."

Suddenly, Caddy screamed again. They heard a crunch in the bow. Before Penny could alter course, the lobster boat shot into the air and onto a rock.

John flew forward. Penny fell back. Caddy screamed and screamed until she saw they were ok. Then she screamed when she saw the hole in the hull.

"John, you're not hurt, are you?" Penny held her head. She was getting tired of steering.

"No." John sloshed through the water filling the cabin. "But Mr. Cavendish is going to kill us. The boat's sinking."

Penny didn't want to worry about that now. "Hurry then."

They scrambled over the deck, onto the rocks and onto the island.

"See – they're all circling the light up there." Penny pointed to the single tree pointing up to the sky.

The air hummed with tiny lights more delicate than mosquitoes. The rain pattered quietly on the rocks. Through the fog, they could smell a fire of driftwood and smoking sea lettuce. Against the green flames, John caught sight of a long shadow.

"Abigail!" John called. "Wait! Don't do anything!"

Three Decisions

"John Tomas?" Abigail swung around. "What are you doing here? It is past your bedtime."

Squint hopped from a tree branch onto his shoulders. "Mrrow," he said in John's ear.

John dug into his pocket. "We have something for you."

Penny dropped the backpack. "And we've got something to say."

John glared at her. "No, we don't."

"Yes, we do."

John didn't let Penny finish. "We found the last stones," he said. "They were in the clock. 'Time gives golden treasures when it is time.' Now it's time." He handed Abigail the stones and opened his backpack. "And I made a new stopper. I think you're supposed to fit the stones in all the spaces. They're pentagons, like the stones. The stopper of that bottle was another clue. It's why The Trader wanted it."

"The Trader?" Abigail stared at John. Smoke from the fire swirled with the fog and the tiny lights. The wind whispered something and Abigail blinked quickly. "John Tomas, I cannot think of what to say. You did not have to come out here, particularly not in this weather. What if something had happened? What would Mr. and Mrs. Davis think?" Abigail's eyes widened. "What will they think? You ought to be with them."

"That's just it." Penny put her hands on her hips. "That's what I was going to say. We shouldn't be with them. They're all wrong."

"No." Abigail's face fell. "I thought they were perfect. You said they were."

"They are perfect. They're better than perfect. That's not it." Penny suddenly felt awkward. "We should have said before. We changed our minds." Penny took a deep breath. "Maybe you shouldn't go."

Abigail blinked. Overhead, the clouds were lifting. Stars were appearing. Then the moon.

Squint jumped from John's shoulder. "Mrrow," he said.

"It's not that we blame you for wanting to leave," Penny told him. "Who'd want to be a cat? And you told us you miss your cottage and everything, Abigail. But you know, if you changed your mind, we'd be glad. Not just John, but me, too."

"But Penelope Rose." Abigail blinked again and again, and then waved smoke from her eyes. "You have had to work so terribly hard these past weeks. And I made mess after mess."

"It was funny," John said.

"It was fun," Penny said.

"But – "

And just then, Abigail slumped to the ground. Squint howled and leaped into the air, but someone batted him against the tree. One squat foot stepped forward and squashed John's copper ball flat.

"No need to thank me," Mal said, tossing an oar aside. "I thought you would be here."

Three Acts of Duty

"What are you doing?" Penny reached for John's hand, but he'd gone to Abigail. "What did you do to Squint? And Abigail?"

"I was just doing my job." Mal pulled a cigar out of her pocket. "The Seleumbrans hired me years ago to be the Keeper, of this area at least. So far, I have kept at least 24 Umbrans going home. A few more and I can retire."

John was confused. "You're from Seleumbra?"

"You are looking at the only brownie on the east coast." Mal squatted down on the ground and regarded Abigail. "I am real grateful that you let me know she had left today. I thought there was nothing to worry about, with you all getting along so well. And I knew Abigail did not have the stopper," Mal pulled out the tiny wire stopper she wore on a string around her neck. "Without it, I figured Abigail had given up."

"You had the stopper." Penny couldn't believe her eyes. "You got it from The Trader. That's why he couldn't give it back."

Mal grunted. "He was no help today. I had to piece things together pretty quick. Finding my way onto the island was a real problem, too. But at least I made it in time. I figure, in about five minutes, it will be too late

214

for Abigail to hitch a ride onto the eclipse." Mal took another bite of her cigar. "I am glad to be doing you a favor at the same time. You are great kids. I always like the scrappy ones. It is lucky that I can give you a hand."

Penny crossed her arms. "We never asked for your help."

"You need it. This Abigail of yours was not about to stay here, no matter how nicely you asked. She used to be one of the best witches in Umbra." Mal spat out the piece of tobacco. "No, I came just in time. You two are lucky."

"Abigail was one of the best witches?" John looked down. Abigail looked pale and sad laying limp on the ground. It wasn't fair, he thought. He had to do something.

"She was famous." Mal took another bite of her cigar. "From what I hear, she was always helping people out of trouble. The Trader still owed her a favor, he said, from their days on on Seleumbra."

"The Trader?" Penny frowned.

"He and your Abigail go way back. He traded at her cottage, long before he got banished here. The Trader said it was the prettiest cottage in Umbra. I bet Abigail misses it." Mal yawned. "But she will have to miss it some more. Look – the eclipse is starting. Keep your eyes down from now on. It is dangerous to watch –"

But just as she turned her head, John flung himself at her. They fell, Mal's face pressed into the dirt. John tried to hold her hands together. "Penny! Quick! Get something to tie her up!"

Penny scrambled for the rope of sea lettuce. "What are you doing?"

"We're sending Abigail home."

215

"Get off me!" Mal writhed and twisted, but John held tight.

Penny threw the rope over Mal's legs and yanked it around her feet. "Hold still," she told her. "You're not going anywhere."

"You can't stop us." John knotted the rope around Mal's hands.

"Let me go." Mal wiggled and tried to break free. "There is no point to this. Neither of you knows what to do —"

"You keep quiet." Penny shoved Abigail's scarf in Mal's mouth. "John has this figured out."

"We have to find the other stones." John began to untie the string from Mal's neck. "Check by the fire."

"Wait a minute." Penny pulled his shoulder to look him in the eye. "You really want to do this? You really want to let Abigail go?"

"It's what she wants." John tugged himself free. "We have to piece the stones together in the stopper. No colors can touch."

Penny took the golden stones from John and found the rest by Abigail's feet. "You'd better do it here in the light. And Mal, you can stop struggling. Mr. Cavendish taught me how to make those knots."

"It's like the puzzle from The Trader." Carefully, John slid the stones into the stopper: red beside white beside green beside gold, and black, again and again. "And we have to boil them with the sea lettuce."

"Abigail has the water boiling already."

John's fingers moved quickly as he thought. He made a mistake with one of the stones, and pried it out. He fit in another and another. But something was wrong. There were too many stones. "You've got to

216

hurry," Penny said, dragging Abigail to the fire. "The light's changing."

John stared at the rocks – 15 rocks for 12 places in the stopper. The colors couldn't touch, just like the puzzle The Trader had given them. The Trader had said he was doing them a favor with the colors of the bottles. He said they might even find it useful.

John rolled the stopper in his hand. He had to have more than three colors, but four colors could fit without touching. So which of the colors was he not supposed to use?

"John, there's not much time."

He swung around. "What were the clues? Do you remember what it said in the living room?"

"'Time gives golden treasures when it is time.'"

"'Fields of rubies hide buried treasure.'"

"I remember. Then there were the ones about losing direction and swirling direction."

"And the one about letting go the ones we found first." John pried out the black stones. "Those aren't real. That's what the clue meant. We have to let the first stones go. It's the other stones that count."

The blue flames licked at the cauldron. Over their heads, ghostly figures floated out of the tree branches and swirled in the smoke. Music had changed into muttering. They were chanting softly, repeating the word, "Seleumbra."

"You've got to hurry, John."

"I know." Red, then green, then white, then gold. Over and over, John dropped the stones in the stopper. The stones began to glow.

"I think it's starting," Penny said, dropping Squint beside Abigail.

Mal fought the ropes harder, but she couldn't move.

"Done!" John fit the last piece in the stopper. The ball of stones shone brighter. John dropped them into the boiling water.

The light sizzled out.

They peered inside the cauldron.

"Oh," John said.

"Didn't it work?" Penny asked.

"I don't know."

Mal tried to say something. The wind through the tree hushed her. And with a blast like a rocket launcher, cauldron spat the concoction into the sky, just as a rim of light appeared out of the fog.

"Don't look!" Penny threw her hands over John's eyes and pulled him onto the ground. All around them, shadows shot up above the trees. The tiny fairies blew past them. The voices sang up from the ocean.

John lifted his head. He had to see.

The air lifted Mal, struggling against the ropes. Squint and Abigail rose, too, gently up into the sky. They lingered a moment in the purple steam. Abigail's head even fell in a sort of nod. Then with a rush of wind, the three flew up into the darkness and into the night.

With another clap like thunder, the sky burst into colors: greens and golds, pinks and shimmery whites. There were all the colors of Abigail's stones.

In a moment, it was over.

Four Together

It was Caddy who guided the Coast Guard to the wreck of Mr. Cavendish's boat. But the next morning it was Mrs. Collins who met them on shore.

"I warned them," Mrs. Collins said, shoving Penny into her car. "Those Davis people thought they knew everything, just because they're famous. But even if Mrs. Davis can talk to a chimpanzee, she cannot assume she's an expert on children. And for all his toys, Trey Davis won't ever understand how you children think. If you think." Mrs. Collins snorted. "So neither of you has made as much as a peep to anyone for explanation. Who are you to run away from a mansion – and go joyriding in a lobster boat? The Coast Guard says you destroyed it. You destroyed any hope of adoption, too, I'll have you know. Mr. and Mrs. Davis think you should go somewhere else. You'll be a better fit there, they said. And I had warned them. I had told them that you were no good. I was right, wasn't I? There's even talk of prison. And now it's raining again. This is the worst day I've ever had."

A shower of rain drenched the car. Over the squeak of the windshield wipers, John could hear a foghorn calling to boats lost at sea. Through the spatters on the windows, Penny could see the street blur into gray clouds. She reached over and took John's hand. She didn't know what was going to happen and it scared her. John pulled his hand away. He didn't know what was going to happen, but he didn't care anymore.

After Mrs. Collins turned off her car, she turned around in her seat. "It's not like I have any alternatives. That girl's home is full, and yesterday I put two boys in the house I had picked out for you, Buster. Bringing you back here was my only option. Maybe that's punishment enough. It's what Mr. and Mrs. Davis told me to do. They thought it was what you wanted."

Penny and John craned their necks to look. They were back again at 47 Postman's Hack.

"Get going," Mrs. Collins said. "Maybe she'll be glad to see you again."

John frowned, but Penny nudged him out of the car. They didn't say anything, even though the house still looked cold and deserted. They didn't say anything when nobody answered the door.

"I suppose she's gone off shell-collecting again," Mrs. Collins said, banging her umbrella against the door. "Typical. As if I didn't have anything else to do today."

"You can leave us here," Penny said. "We'll wait. You can come back later when you have the time."

John scanned Penny's face. She sounded innocent, but with a glance, she warned him to keep still.

"Fine," Mrs. Collins said. "You have a key? I'll be back this afternoon with more papers for Miss McKinney to sign. You tell her that. And Mr. and Mrs. Davis said they'd come with your things a little later once you've settled." The ceiling above the porch creaked and hurriedly, Mrs. Collins put up her umbrella. "I'll be back by four."

Penny and John didn't move until Mrs. Collins drove away.

"What are we going to do?" John asked. "Stay here?"

Penny shrugged. "We might as well until the weather clears up. Then we'd better go down to the beach. We have to explain to Mr. Cavendish."

"He's going to be mad."

"He should be mad."

John peered through a window. "I'm hungry," he said. "Do you think there's any food left?"

Penny shook the door. "We might have to break in. The door won't budge."

"We could smash a window —"

The door swung open. Penny and John froze.

"Hello?" Penny called.

Nobody answered. They waited and still, nobody answered.

"Maybe Mr. Cavendish is back," Penny said. "Hello?"

Nobody answered.

"Abigail said it could be haunted."

"The house isn't haunted, dope."

Suddenly, a hairy arm shot out from behind the door. It grabbed John and tossed him up to the ceiling. "Bleach my shirts and blacken my boots!" shouted the owner of the arm. "You are no bigger than a pipsqueak!"

The man put John down. "And I have some words to say to you, Penelope Rose. Dogs! I think not!"

Penny and John stared at him. Short and round, with tufts of black hair and an empty, scarred eye, the man flashed a gold tooth at them. "Come on now," the man said. "Surely, you recognize me."

221

"Captain Zach?" John asked tentatively.

"Right in the first go!" Captain Zach whisked John up into the air again. "Send me away, do you, when a man is no well aware of his surroundings? It was hardly fair not to ask my opinion, which is not to say I am not grateful. It is mighty good to be back in my bones again."

Penny slumped back against the doorway. "How –"

"How indeed?" And there was Abigail, beaming as she came out of the kitchen. "Penelope Rose, how did you know to come greet us? John Tomas, it is good to see you again."

John threw himself at her. Penny almost felt like crying.

"You came back!"

"Why?"

"You wanted to go home."

"We thought you didn't want to stay."

Abigail laughed delightedly. "There was no question that I wanted to stay. I never would have left last night if Mal had not interrupted things. But of course, I am very grateful to you both for defending us."

"As am I," Captain Zach said with a flourish. "Even more so, considering the circumstances."

"When Zach and I came to our senses in Seleumbra, we had a long conversation," Abigail said. "That is, we talked after I had restored him."

"—To my non-feline self." Captain Zach made a little bow.

"We discussed what would be the best course to take. If we had believed that you had found the perfect family, we would have let you go to Mr. and Mrs. Davis without complaining."

"With visits on occasion," Captain Zach interrupted, "for inspection purposes."

"You children had said that you would prefer to keep our family together – in spite of fires and mishaps and mayhem." Abigail squeezed Penny's hand. "And when we talked it over, the decision was easy to make. Almost immediately, here we were again."

"And we can stay together?" John asked.

"We can stay together." Abigail tussled his hair.

"Together a family!" Captain Zach declared, pulling a pistol from his belt. Before Abigail could stop him, he shot at the ceiling. Sparks flew from the chandelier. It crashed to the floor.

"Really, Zach." Abigail turned on him. "Was that necessary? Mr. Cavendish just fixed the wiring. Now we will have to ask him to do it again."

"We have to tell to him you're back," Penny said. "We should go right now. He thought he'd never see you again."

John felt guilty all of a sudden. "We have to talk to him anyway. We crashed his boat. It's pretty bad."

Penny started to worry, too. "Mr. and Mrs. Davis aren't so happy with us either."

"We ran away."

"The Coast Guard had to rescue us again."

"Mrs. Collins said we might go to jail."

"Tan my hide and bury my body!" Captain Zach stomped his foot. "No problems before my breakfast. I want an egg – on a real plate this time. Today, I am going to eat with a fork!"

A puff of black smoke wafted from the kitchen.

"I am sorry, Penelope Rose," Abigail said. "I must have forgotten to turn down the oven."

"Blast it." Captain Zach stuffed his pistol into his pants and marched down the hallway. "You had better not have burned my bacon."

"You can make your own bacon now," Abigail called after him. They heard a crack and then a crash. "Stop shooting at the stove!"

"Don't worry." Penny headed to the kitchen. "I'll fix it. French toast, right?"

They heard another shot and a spurt of water.

Abigail's shoulders dropped. "Oh, dear," she said again.

John laughed. It was good to be home.

Made in the USA
Lexington, KY
10 May 2010